In *Confessions to a Stranger*, Danielle Grandinetti weaves a tale that is at once mysterious, suspenseful, romantic, and inspiring ... Filled with truths that made me ponder my own life, this novel is a lovely start to what is sure to be a wonderful series!

—Heidi Chiavaroli,
Carol Award-Winning Author of *The Orchard House*

Danielle Grandinetti has crafted a wonderful tale of suspense and romance that will keep you on the edge of your seat. With well-drawn characters authentic to the era, a gripping plot, and a strong message of hope, *Confessions to a Stranger* is a read I recommend!

—Misty M. Beller,
USA Today bestselling author of the Sisters of the Rockies

A Strike to the Heart is a compelling story. From the very first page, I was immersed into the thrilling action and remained gripped with intrigue until the satisfying ending. The romance escalated right along with the winding plot, creating a layered mystery that is sure to delight readers.

—Rachel Scott McDaniel,
Award-winning author of *The Mobster's Daughter*

Riveting from the first scene, *As Silent as the Night* offers a unique, edge-of-your-seat Christmas read ... A beautiful, gripping, and romantically suspenseful Christmas story you wouldn't be able to put down if you tried.

—Chautona Havig,
Author of *The Stars of New Cheltenham*

The Neighbor and the Gifts is a poignant tale that transforms a familiar carol into a stirring journey of faith, love, and danger ... For readers who love historical romance, mystery, and want a deeper meaning in their holiday stories—this one's for you.

—Natalie Walters,
bestselling and award-winning author of *Living Lies* and the *SNAP Agency* series

Heart of Beauty

**Discover the Foundation
of Danielle's Bookish World**

Harbored in Crow's Nest
Confessions to a Stranger
Refuge for the Archaeologist
Escape with the Prodigal
Relying on the Enemy
Sheltered by the Doctor
Investigation of a Journalist

Bridge: His Boss's Little Sister

Unexpected Protectors
To Stand in the Breach
A Strike to the Heart
As Silent as the Night

For a complete list, visit
daniellegrandinetti.com/books

Heart of Beauty

Danielle Grandinetti

Hearth Spot Press

HEART OF BEAUTY

Copyright © 2025 by Danielle Grandinetti

Published by Hearth Spot Press

Kindle Book ISBN: 978-1-956098-24-2

Paperback ISBN (1): 978-1-956098-25-9

Paperback ISBN (2): 978-1-956098-43-3

All rights reserved.

No part of this publication may be reproduced, distributed, or transmitted in any form or by any means, including photocopying, recording, or other electronic or mechanical methods, without the prior written permission of the publisher, with the exception of limited quotations for use in reviews or promotional material or as permitted by U.S. copyright law. Neither may any unauthorized use of this publication be used to train generative artificial intelligence (AI) technologies. For permission requests, contact the author at daniellegrandinetti.com/contact.

The story, all names, characters, and incidents portrayed in this production are fictitious. No identification with actual persons (living or deceased), places, buildings, and products is intended or should be inferred.

In memory of Betty Helgeson

My grandmother-in-law, fellow book-lover,

and a graduate of Polson High School in Polson, Montana.

And let the beauty of the Lord our God be upon us:

and establish thou the work of our hands upon us;

yea, the work of our hands establish thou it.

Psalm 90:17, KJV

Chapter One

March 15, 1871

Heart of Montana Territory

"Beware the Ides of March," Sallie Beauregard muttered as she donned the disguise within her room, tucking her long braid up inside her cowboy hat. In Shakespeare's day, young men played female roles in his plays. Here in Montana Territory, she dressed as a boy to keep wayward eyes from realizing she was, in fact, a very eligible maiden.

"Sal, you ready, my girl?" her father called from the main room. A well-respected nomad trapper, it'd been his idea to dress her in trousers and a buckskin coat after Mama died when Sallie was but a child of five. Sallie hadn't minded then. It was easier to traipse after her father in something other than a dress. Who had use for frills and lace, anyway?

She still believed that, but now she wore plain dresses or a split skirt unless they went into a town. Then she honored her father's request because all anyone knew of old Saul Beauregard, who lived up on the mountain near Blue Spruce, Montana, was that he had a son named Sal—a son who never spoke—except to horses.

Sallie slung her saddlebags over her shoulder as she followed her father to the barn. "Where are we making camp tonight?"

With the first breaths of spring, Papa got antsy to leave the confines of the old cabin. They'd return every few weeks to stock up on supplies, then go again to hunt and sell the meat and furs to those in towns along their way.

Papa scratched his full gray beard. "We'll head down to the valley and follow the waking critters."

She nodded. There was no need to comment as she saddled Gunpowder, named for the horse Ichabod Crane rode in Washington Irving's tale. When she first met Gunpowder, the poor horse reminded her of the broken-down plow horse in the book. She patted his nose. Now his black coat shone, and his belly showed him well-fed. Gunpowder nuzzled her under the chin.

Supplies loaded onto the horses, she swung into the saddle and followed Papa down the mountain. Today, she believed spring could be around the corner. While a chill still permeated the air, snow dripped from the cabin roof and rocky outcroppings. Soon, the rivers would rage, waking the world from the depth of winter.

The advent of warmer weather usually sparked warmth in her heart, but a strange foreboding hovered this year. Perhaps because they were setting out on the fifteenth of March? She might not be superstitious, but she loved her books and had read *Julius Caesar* a few too many times not to have the warning echo in her head.

She rubbed Gunpowder's neck, letting a prayer from Psalm 121 whisper upon the wind. *The Lord shall preserve thy going out and thy coming in from this time forth, and even for evermore. Amen.*

The journey down the mountain took several hours, and they paused for the noon meal before entering the town limits. The cowboys and miners who happened to be in Blue Spruce greeted Papa warmly. They traded gossip as much as legitimate news. Sallie listened as she gathered canned goods in the general store. She recognized a few names from their last visit. Some had given up their claims and headed back east or further west. But one name stood out. It never ceased to send shivers down her spine.

Physically large and politically powerful, Brendan Doran thought first only of himself. Perhaps that's why he owned the largest saloon in town, a place that also housed the only other unmarried women who lived in Blue Spruce. And the primary reason Papa disguised Sallie's femininity.

"Rumor is Doran wants to settle down." One grizzled man set a tin of tobacco on the counter. "Can you imagine having all those women around you and wanting to pick just one to spend the rest of your life with?"

Another old cowboy tipped up his hat and laughed. "I doubt he'll give that up. He just needs a girl he can hoodwink."

Papa caught Sallie's eye, nodded toward the crate of goods he was about to pay for, and then pointed his chin toward the door. He wanted her away from this conversation, and Sallie was more than happy to oblige.

She shouldered the crate as a lad might and pushed into the pale sunlight. The men who passed barely cast her a second glance. Just as she set the crate beside where she and Papa had tied the horses, a shout brought her gaze east, to the road leading out of Blue Spruce. Or into it, considering the billowing cloud that loomed closer.

Sallie rested her hand on Gunpowder's flank as she circled him. Men ran out of buildings as a horse with a black coat that made Gunpowder's color appear faded galloped into town, a lead rope trailing behind him. Considering the rope's frayed end, the black must have broken his lead. And having it whacking his bare back surely wasn't helping his panic. Fortunately, the horse slowed as it reached the center of town, but his nostrils flared.

Mr. Doran swaggered out of his saloon, laughing loudly. "Orson can't even keep hold of his horse." Doran weaved as he walked, probably inebriated.

The black, presumably owned by local reclusive rancher Caleb Orson, shied. Sallie could see what would happen next as if reading it in the pages of her favorite book.

"Wait! It's the horse Orson stole from me!" Doran added colorful descriptions that burned Sallie's ears as he strode toward the animal. His cocky bluster propelled her into Gunpowder's saddle, leaving the crate of supplies beside Papa's horse.

"It's not your horse, Doran!" someone shouted.

"Leave him alone!" another man shouted.

Sallie cringed but put Gunpowder into motion, aiming in the direction she suspected the black would run: west, toward the mountains.

Doran pulled his pistol, though what he planned to do with it was anyone's guess. "This horse cost me—"

The black horse reared and then ran.

She and Gunpowder were already in place, cantering in the same direction the black raced. At any moment, she expected a gunshot to strike the air or a bullet to whiz by as the black horse caught up to them by the edge of town. *Lord, Your protection, please!*

Galloping side by side, not chasing, she hoped her horse could calm the black so she could get him away from Doran.

Except a large cowboy astride a gigantic horse thundered toward them from the south. Orson. She recognized him by his horse, and the beard that hid most of his face. He must have circled the outskirts of town, aiming to cut off the black. It would have worked, if Doran hadn't spooked the poor animal.

Behind them, an angry Doran had jumped on a horse and given chase, pistol free of his holster. Would he shoot a horse in broad daylight? Risk a hanging? If he was drunk enough, maybe he hadn't thought it through.

Of course, the hoopla only made the black gallop faster. He veered northwest toward the open plain that rose to meet the mountains, away from both his master and Doran. Gunpowder kept pace beside him, the two running as a herd, even with Sallie on Gunpowder's back.

"It's going to be just fine, ol' boy," she said, bending low over Gunpowder's neck. *Please, Lord.* Her body, tense from expecting a gunshot, ached with the ride. But she wouldn't let the black face this danger alone.

Gunpowder kept pace with the black, whose sides were heaving now. How long had the horse been running before reaching town? And what had caused it to spook so that it ran so far from home? All questions for after she got the poor beast to stop.

Using Gunpowder, she guided the black toward the mountain path she and Papa had used less than an hour ago. The rising ground caused the horse to slow enough that Sallie felt it safe enough to grab the broken lead rope and give a gentle tug.

"Whoa there, ol' boy." She spoke firmly, banking that the authority in her voice would give the black a sense of security. "Whoa, now. You've run enough."

The black slowed more, and when they came to the edge of the mountain, instead of picking its way up the path, the horse turned and halted. Late afternoon sunlight cast them in the shadow of the cliff face. The black tossed his head and pawed the ground. Sallie slid from Gunpowder's back and tiptoed into the black's line of sight. He snorted and huffed.

"Easy, ol' boy. You poor thing. Utterly terrified, aren't you?" She eased closer, the rope still in her hand. A frothy, heaving mass of muscle he was. "What spooked you, huh? Was it a little critter or a big one? Human or animal? Hmm? You can tell me, ol' boy."

The black shook his head.

"Not talking, huh? That's all right. No need to relive what scared you so." She held out her hand, palm up. "But I'm here now and won't let anything harm you."

Eyes wide, he backed up a step. Sallie didn't move. Didn't speak. Just waited. Another snort came from the horse. Gunpowder nosed at the slushy ground for any grass that might appear beneath the melting snow.

Pounding hooves gave warning that they'd have company in moments, spooking the horse again. Only then did she realize her tactical error. She never spoke when she went into a town, especially when they went into Blue Spruce. She might disguise her figure, but her voice was undeniably that of a woman.

If Arion, or the lad who went chasing after the black horse, were injured, Caleb Orson could blame no one but himself. If only he'd realized he used a frayed rope when he tied Arion in the open yard. If only that stack of boards hadn't fallen so near him. If only ... well, there were only so many regrets a man could have.

Usually, when one of his horses got out, they stayed close, but Arion's fear sent him searching for his old herd. At least, that's what Caleb suspected. He'd rescued the horse when he was injured a year ago, then tried to release him back into the wild. If Doran would have left the poor animal alone, maybe all would have gone well. But the man had wanted to break the majestic animal and now had a vendetta.

Caleb didn't trust what Doran would do if he came upon Arion alone. Or if only a boy stood in his way. He was too powerful in town. No one would speak against him to the marshal.

Arion and the lad halted at the cliff face west of Blue Spruce, but Doran chased them. Caleb had attempted to intercept while his foreman and one of his cowboys followed Arion from behind. The plan had been to herd Arion back toward the ranch after the horse cleared the town. If only …

The lad had slid down from his horse. Fear for the youth pumped through his body so that the blood pulsing in his ears blended with the pounding of his horse's hooves. *Your fault. Your fault.* The lad glanced over his shoulder, obviously spotting Doran's approach.

Arion snorted and shied. His fear edged toward panic. If Doran spooked Arion, this could become a deadly situation. Caleb adjusted his grip on Duke's reigns, unsure how to save this situation.

"What's the plan, boss?" Art Thomas, his foreman, came alongside. "Doran is going to get that kid killed."

The lad edged between Arion and his own horse, a large black one not nearly as sleek as the stallion. Caleb's stomach vaulted into his chest. Broken bodies swam in his memory. Blue uniforms and gray. Friends and enemies.

"Sal!" The shout cleared the fog from before his eyes and made him aware of the heaviness of his breathing. And then the melee before him.

Arion kicked at the air. The lad ducked before his slashing hooves. The lad's horse pranced sideways. Saul Beauregard galloped past them, catching up to Doran, who had slowed at the trapper's shout. What was the old man thinking? Wait. Was the kid the trapper's son? The one who would only speak to horses?

Arion reared, and the boy stepped out of the horse's way, letting it take off south along the range. Defeat washed the other emotions from inside Caleb. Hopefully, Arion wouldn't run far. Maybe even circle back to the ranch. He'd give him a minute, make sure the lad wasn't hurt. Maybe confront Doran for pulling a pistol aimed at the horse.

He, Thomas, and the newest addition to his ranch, fifteen-year-old Carl Anchorman, reined to a stop beside Beauregard and Doran.

"That horse is a menace, Orson." The sneer was Doran's greeting. "Or are you such a beast that all critters just run away from you?"

Caleb clenched his jaw and fisted his hands around Duke's reins. When Doran first arrived in Blue Spruce wearing the tattered trousers of a blue Union uniform, Caleb thought they would be friends. Brothers-in-arms. But Doran was mean, and greedy, and that was putting it kindly.

"Unless you plan to help us herd Caleb's horse, move along, Doran," Thomas spoke with an emotionless authority Caleb could never have achieved.

Still, he pulled Thomas back with a shake of his head and pointed his chin toward where Arion had disappeared. Caleb wouldn't let Thomas get caught in Doran's sights. Thomas backed away.

"You don't deserve that critter. If I catch up to it again, I'm taking the shot." Doran glared at Caleb, and Caleb knew the man would do exactly that.

"No!" The lad pushed between them, facing down Doran as if he didn't tower above him. "That horse doesn't deserve to die because of your feud with Mr. Orson."

Doran's laugh faded at the same moment the realization struck Caleb. Sal Beauregard wasn't the old trapper's son. Sal was his *daughter*.

Chapter Two

"Look what you've done." Papa groaned as he dismounted at Sallie's side.

She tried to hold up her chin, but how Doran eyed her threatened to take the starch out of her spine. It made her feel like one of Papa's pelts. And she didn't like it. Not one bit. No wonder Papa insisted she pretended to be a boy. She edged behind Papa's shoulder, wishing she hadn't spoiled everything with her outburst.

But the man wanted to kill an animal for a reason other than survival! Never.

"Enough Doran." Caleb Orson growled from behind them. "Unless you plan on helping me bring my horse home, get back to whatever you were doing."

Doran just laughed. "What if I want to meet the lady? It is a pleasure to make your acquaintance, Miss Beauregard." He dismounted and tipped his cowboy hat toward her.

"It is most assuredly not a pleasure, sir." She edged further behind Papa.

"Leave her alone, Mr. Doran." Papa folded his arms.

But Doran dwarfed Papa as much as he ignored him. "I like you, little lady. You've got spunk. I've been looking for a missus and you would do right fine."

Of all the—

"Back off, Doran." Orson stepped beside Papa, creating a protective wall between her and Doran's leering. When had he gotten off his horse? She hadn't heard him, and surely someone who out-matched Doran in size would have made a sound.

"Like you have a chance, Orson." Doran laughed, but Sallie could find no humor in it. "Beauregard, I'll take the girl off your hands for the price of a wedding ceremony. What do you say?"

Sallie's jaw dropped. The man was trying to bargain as if she were nothing but a horse to be traded for? She would never—never!—agree to marry a stuck-up man like that.

"I say no, Mr. Doran." How did Papa keep such a level tone? Sallie planted her hands on her hips only to have her shoulder nudged from behind. She glanced back at the horse ridden by Mr. Orson. A tan gelding with a dark brown mane. Beautiful creature. She patted his cheek, gaining comfort.

"Like anyone can turn me down." Doran's gaze found Sallie's between the men, and she wanted to run like the black stallion had done. Away. Far, far away. With a crooked grin that said he'd get his way eventually, Doran mounted his horse and left them without another word.

Sallie shivered—not from the encroaching evening—and leaned into the tan gelding as if the animal could protect her. Her fingers tangled in his mane. Why hadn't she realized the danger of losing her disguise?

"What were you thinking?" The snapping words came not from her father but from Mr. Orson. Like a knife, they pierced without regard. "You don't chase a horse. He could have killed you. And now Doran knows you're a female. Could you be more ... witless?"

Sallie raised her chin. "Pardon me for helping, Mr. Orson." Horses didn't scare her. They gave her courage.

But Mr. Orson didn't back down. She gave the gelding one more pat, then stepped toe-to-toe with the large man. His height forced her to look up, up his broad chest, to find his burning green eyes.

"I had the situation well under control if it wasn't for you men."

Had she really said that out loud? Her father huffed, but Mr. Orson simply stared at her. Fine. She'd handled bears before, but was Mr. Orson a black bear or a grizzly? Stuff and nonsense. With a huff, she spun on her heel and marched toward Gunpowder. She'd find his horse—Arion, he'd called him—and return him safely to Orson's ranch. All on her own.

"Sal!" Papa called after her, but Sallie was too churned up inside to listen. Without waiting for an answer from Mr. Orson or even permission from Papa, she swung into the saddle and set off at a canter.

Gunpowder edged toward a gallop, obviously sensing her tension. That wouldn't do. She closed her eyes, giving Gunpowder his head, and breathed in the damp mountain air. Rain was on the darkening horizon. Maybe snow, seeing as the chill deepened with the sun's setting.

From the rising of the sun unto the going down of the same The LORD's name is to be praised. The words from Psalm 113 roamed through her mind.

Her eyes snapped open. She didn't feel much like praising God right now. No, sir. Why couldn't a verse about vengeance have crossed her mind? She had most of the Psalms memorized, seeing how long the winters kept her and Papa isolated at the cabin. Not much else to do other than read, which meant she'd reread all the books she owned more times than she could remember, including the old family Bible.

The righteous shall rejoice when he seeth the vengeance was a good verse from Psalm 58. She would rejoice if a man like Doran got what was coming to him. Trying to buy her like a piece of property. Of all the—

"You're going to wear down your horse at this pace." When had Mr. Orsen caught up to her? She usually had more awareness than this, but he was so ... silent. Except when he yelled at her.

"What's it to you?" she snapped, then rolled her eyes. "Sorry."

"And it won't do to chase Arion like we're hunting him." Mr. Orson ignored her outburst, which was unexpectedly kind of him. "My foreman is following the horse at a discreet distance."

She relaxed her hands on the reins, and Gunpowder slowed a hair. Maybe she had overreacted. "Where's Papa?"

"Went to pack up the supplies you unceremoniously left outside the general store." Was that censure in his voice?

Sallie narrowed her eyes. Maybe he wasn't so kind. "Mince words, why don't you?"

He shrugged a massive shoulder. "Don't see the need to waste 'em."

Sallie pinned her lips together rather than allow the retort out of her mouth. Instead, she studied this man whose horse they tracked, attempting to get his measure. She'd heard the rumors that he was an angry, solitary soldier. Some said he murdered a man and was hiding from the law. Others said he lost his love and was nursing a broken heart. Her father's Blackfoot friend, Ahanu, insisted that Mr. Orson was a wounded soul but a good man.

Wishing to make her own opinions and having only seen him from a distance a few times, she began with an outward assessment. Brown hair curled against the woolen collar of his buckskin coat. A brown beard bushier than Papa's covered his face. His cowboy hat had the look of one well-loved and often used. His clothing was also much like Papa's, especially the buckskin trousers with fringe along the seams. And the boots. The worn, faded, scuffed cowboy boots.

"Approve of what you see, miss?" The grumbly voice held no amusement.

Embarrassment flashed through her as she jerked her gaze to his eyes. Was that a twinkle? Couldn't be. The man seemed gruff and not in the habit of being around genteel company. Or any company, considering the rumors. But she and her father weren't much different, were they? Nomadic versus solitary—both meant being alone. Maybe she had more in common with this bear of a man.

She focused on where two saddled horses gave evidence to the companions Mr. Orson mentioned. Realization struck. She was in the middle of the wilderness with three unknown men and without Papa or a chaperone. Could she believe Ahanu's assessment? Were these men like Mr. Doran, or did her honor have a hope of escaping without injury?

Not that she'd back down in the face of making sure an animal survived. She'd finish her quest. See that the black horse—Arion—would be well cared for, whether by returning to Orson's ranch or bartering the animal from him.

Resolve setting her spine, she ignored the large man riding beside her and studied the scene ahead. The two cowboys had the tired horse pinned between them and the rock face. The poor animal reared, its eyes large and white, even from here. She'd have a time of it, getting the stallion to calm. If only they had a paddock nearby where she could ease her way into Arion's good graces. No time for that now. She'd have to earn enough trust that the horse would allow her to see him safely home.

"Stay back, miss." The grumble came from her left.

Sallie rolled her eyes. "Might as well be hung for a colt as for a stallion."

"Pardon?" This time, the grumble had turned to a growl.

Sallie reined in Gunpowder with a huff. "Hung for a lamb as for a sheep. In for a penny, in for a pound. I'm here; might as well make the most of it." She swung down before the man could protest.

"The Lord shall preserve thy going out and thy coming in from this time forth." She whispered the words that had brought comfort this morning as she approached the terrified stallion. "And even for evermore."

Who did this woman think she was? Caleb swung down from Duke's back. His long legs ate up the ground between her and him, allowing him to reach for her arm before she got as far as the horse. Thomas and the kid, Anchorman, had Arion cornered. They could handle getting Arion home. No need to endanger Beauregard's daughter. He shook his head. *Daughter?*

Caleb jerked her to a stop with fingers hooked around her arm. She spun at the momentum shift he caused, her hand landing on his chest to keep herself from falling. The set of her jaw had him backing up, out of range of the hand she balled into a fist. This woman knew how to fight.

"I don't reckon answering to your father if you get hurt." He folded his arms, letting his barrel chest expand. Not that his attempt at intimidation would work on her. Sal—*Sallie*—Beauregard seemed impervious to such things. It made him curious, a feeling that just made him more irritable.

"I thank you for that, but I take full responsibility." She nodded as if that ended the conversation and spun on her toe.

Thomas met Caleb's eye over his shoulder, asking for direction. Frankly, he had no idea. The woman wouldn't listen to reason. But she was the lad known for his way of speaking to horses. The connection twisted in his head, and a growl rumbled out of him.

Miss Beauregard pressed steepled hands to her mouth, which drew his attention to what he'd never noticed about her before: her beauty. When he thought her a trapper's son, he didn't think twice about her straight figure or ruddy complexion. Now he noticed her long lashes and the thin lips within her perfectly round face. It was enough to fan his irritation to full-fledged anger. Romance was for a good man, and Caleb had no blinders to the fact he was not one.

"Thomas, keep the horse there. I'll grab his lead and—" Caleb bit off his words when Miss Beauregard jabbed her palm at him.

Without a word, she glided toward Arion, moving as if she wore a ball gown, not boys' trousers. She stopped one step closer to Arion than Thomas and Anchorman. Arion reared. The men, including Caleb, stepped back. Miss Beauregard did not.

"I know, I know," she crooned, "you've had a dreadful fright. How very far you've run today. I'm sure you're tired and hungry. Thirsty, too. I don't have any treats for you."

Arion snorted but didn't rear.

"Ah, you like the idea of a treat, do you?" She leaned closer as if sharing a secret. "I do, too. In fact, huckleberry pie is my favorite. You probably prefer oats. Yes?"

Caleb exchanged another glance with Thomas. What was she doing? Talking to Arion like a child would not bring the horse back to the ranch. And Caleb considered Duke his best friend.

"I'm sure we can find you some oats." The woman prattled like an Easterner. "That will be just the thing for you. And definitely good clean water. Don't you think that sounds like a wonderful treat?"

"Miss," Thomas mumbled.

Miss Beauregard ever so slightly turned her shoulder to Caleb's right-hand man and in doing so, took a step toward Arion. Caleb shifted his weight to his toes, ready to scoop her out of the way should Arion react. With her slightness, he should have no trouble tossing her out of Arion's path.

"I'd like nothing better than a cool sip of spring water. All this racing around has made me parched." Had she inched closer to the horse? "My canteen water is likely cool. Don't you feel the chill in the air?"

Now that she mentioned it, yes, he did. He also realized the sun had set behind the mountains, leaving a yellow glow. It was not a proper sunset yet, but it was enough to cast long shadows here. And what did Miss Beauregard plan to do with night hastening? Now everyone knew she was an unmarried woman, which left her reputation at risk. All for a horse. A valuable one, one Caleb was willing to risk life and limb for, but why should she?

"That's it, Arion. That's your name, isn't it? Like the horse from the Greek stories. Such a sad tale, don't you think?" She reached her hand toward Arion's cheek.

Caleb's muscles coiled, but when Arion stretched his neck toward her, he froze.

"Ah, you like stories, do you?" Miss Beauregard trailed fingers along Arion's face until she grasped the broken lead rope.

Let the world be still, just for a moment. The thought flitted through his mind like a goldfinch. Was it a prayer? He hadn't uttered one of those since Spotsylvania when the screams of dying men echoed in his ears. What if Arion reared with Miss Beauregard so close? One more person couldn't die because of him.

Chapter Three

Sallie fought off the tension radiating around her. Arion would read it in her if she allowed it to affect her. They couldn't afford a step backward. Night was darkening the sky too quickly. For both her safety and Arion's, they needed to get the horse back home.

"Do you want to tell these gentlemen the plan, or shall I?" She spoke to Arion but raised her voice to be heard by the three men behind her. "I'm just going to take your lead. Yes, you'll be right next to me and Gunpowder the whole time. No need to fret."

Shifting feet almost tugged her attention to what was happening behind her, but she pinned her gaze on the horse, hovering her palm over his neck.

"And if you'll allow it, Sir Arion, your master will be on your right. You'll be safe between us." She closed her fingers over the reins. "We'll go nice and slow, but soon you'll be snug in your stall with plenty of food and water."

"Mount up, boys." Mr. Orson's muted command caused activity behind her. She kept her back to them to keep Arion focused on her—crooning words telling what the horse could expect as they rode home. Then Mr. Orson brought her Gunpowder's reins.

"As soon as we go, I need one person in the lead so I know where I'm going. Arion sets the pace." She didn't have time to make her words sound less like orders. Hopefully, the men's pride wouldn't undo everything she'd accomplished with Arion.

"You heard her. Anchorman, lead the way." Mr. Orson moved his horse to Arion's right side. He listened! This grumbly, muscled man listened to her. No time to dwell on it. Sallie pushed the shock of it away and swung into her saddle.

The movement caused Arion to flare his nostrils and paw the ground. Keeping hold of his lead, she gave him his head and urged Gunpowder to keep pace. The younger cowboy—Mr. Anchorman—led the way. The older cowboy rode a bit behind. Between her and Mr. Orson, they kept Arion at the center of the herd. Safe. Calm. And headed home.

By the time the shadowy form of a sprawling ranch rose from the horizon, stars dotted the dark sky. Arion would need to be watched closely after his escapades and checked for injury. A list ran through Sallie's mind as she followed the younger cowboy through the open yard toward a maze of fencing. Shouts went up, and a corral gate was opened that sent Arion through to the stable.

"You." Mr. Orson pointed at a cowboy. "See that these horses get a good rub down."

Sallie kept Gunpowder at a walk, circling the yard. How far was it to town? "I need to get back and find my father."

Mr. Orson shook his head as he dismounted and handed his reins to a waiting cowboy. "It's too late, Miss Beauregard. Town is no place for a young lady at this time of evening. And your horse is done in."

Sallie's nerves jangled despite the truth of his words. Gunpowder came to a halt. "I can't very well stay here, Mr. Orson."

Mr. Orson huffed and waved at the older cowboy who had ridden in with them. "My foreman, Art Thomas." The gray-haired man tipped his cap and then swung to the ground. Slower than Mr. Orson but with a grace that belied his age.

"No offense, sir, but he is not enough to be my chaperone here." Sallie wove her fingers in Gunpowder's mane and rubbed his neck.

Mr. Thomas chuckled. "None taken. But Caleb was referring to my wife. Maggie. We'd be honored to have you join us this evening, and she'd be right pleased to have another woman around for the evening."

Oh, well then. "Um. I suppose I don't have much choice." But Papa would be worried sick. Would he be scouring the area for her? He knew she took off after Arion, so would he think to look here? Did he expect her to return to town? If only she knew how to get him word that she was okay.

"Good. I'll see you in the morning." Mr. Orson strode to the house without a backward glance.

Of all the—

"Don't let him get to you, miss." Mr. Thomas waved her down from Gunpowder. "He's a good man underneath all the thorns. The boys will see to your horse. Come meet my missus."

Having no protest, Sallie handed off Gunpowder, shouldered her saddlebags, and followed the bowlegged man toward a small structure near the stable. It was in sight of the main house and the bunkhouses behind the stable, yet it had a cozy cabin feel that reminded her of home. A warm yellow light shone through the front window, and smoke rose from the chimney. As soon as Mr. Thomas opened the front door, a melody sung by a beautiful voice swept out, causing Mr. Thomas's weathered face to brighten.

"That's my missus. A right nightingale, she is." He waved Sallie inside before hailing his wife. "I brought us a visitor, Maggie Sweet."

"Oh?" The sturdy woman turned from the washbasin, a towel in her hands. She wore her gray hair in a long braid over her shoulder. She patted her worn apron as if she could smooth over the water splatters. "Heavens, I'm not dressed for visitors. Who is this?"

"Trapper Beauregard's daughter, Sallie."

"Daughter?" Mrs. Thomas's jaw dropped for a moment, but she recovered quickly, crossing the room to scoop Sallie's hands in her rough ones. "I'm sorry, I never noticed. My eyes must be failing. You're as pretty as a sunrise."

Sallie knew her cheeks must have turned red. She freed her hands to set her saddlebags on the floor against her leg. "Papa desired to keep me safe, ma'am. We didn't mean to fool people. Though, I suppose we did. It's just—"

Mrs. Thomas waved her quiet. "It makes perfect sense, dear. Now, when was the last time you ate? When Caleb didn't return in time for supper, I had no choice but to divvy up the food to avoid wasting it."

Sallie's stomach rumbled in answer, and Mrs. Thomas laughed, then sent her to wash up.

After a delightful conversation over a delicious meal, Mr. and Mrs. Thomas retired, explaining their early morning. Sallie knew she should sleep as well, but after the day, she couldn't rest just yet.

Mrs. Thomas had her set up in the back bedroom of their cabin. It doubled as the sick room so the older lady could serve as a nurse, but she assured Sallie it had been thoroughly cleaned since the last cowboy had been injured. Sallie believed it as she smoothed the quilt and the fresh scent of sunshine wafted from the fabric.

Lord, be with Papa tonight. The prayer brought her to the window. She ran her finger over the glass. In their cabin up the mountain, they had a single window. The story went that Papa cut it out of the wall and fit it with the precious glass the summer Mama's illness rendered her bedridden. Her dying wish had been to close her eyes upon the sun here on earth and wake in Heaven's glorious light.

Mr. Orson must be a prosperous rancher to allow his ranch supervisor to have multiple windows in his house. Or perhaps this window served the same purpose it had for Mama. Hope for the sick.

Movement caught her gaze, and she squinted to make it out. Based on the confident stride, plus the height and breadth of his build, it must be Mr. Orson. He roved from building to building.

He checked fences and secured doors. Things his cowhands would have seen to before they retired for the night. He glanced toward the Thomases' house, then rechecked the same fences and doors he'd checked before.

Rumors of Caleb Orson's reclusive ways came to mind. Jokes about him being a beast. Angry. Sullen. Silent. The men in Blue Spruce didn't seem to have much good to say about this rancher, yet the jealousy she'd always detected caused her to suspect their criticisms. Now, she had the opportunity to see whether they were right or whether Mr. Orson was simply misunderstood. Mr. and Mrs. Thomas, and Papa's friend Ahanu, thought Mr. Orson a good man. So, who was her reticent host? And what made him that way?

Caleb's breath puffed out in a white cloud as he left the cattle barn to intercept Thomas. Snow had fallen in the wee hours of the morning. Light snow that blew through the air like a fine, icy mist that left layered the world with a sparkle Caleb didn't feel.

"How's the cow?" Thomas swung down from his horse and pointed his chin toward the door Caleb had just left.

"Irritable." Caleb crossed his arms. During Caleb's sleepless wandering last night, he spotted the expectant animal, and instincts warned him something was wrong. He just didn't know what yet. "Did you find Beauregard?"

A cowhand appeared, and Thomas handed off his reins. "I did. He sent me back with instructions."

"Instructions for what?" What did the man mean to do? He had already let his daughter go off on her own with no assurance of her safety. And with Doran's lecherous proposal, it not only made no sense, it was downright dangerous.

"Seems he thinks he knows his daughter better than we do." Thomas stuffed his hands into the pockets of his buckskin coat and turned for the stable. "Shall we see if he's correct?"

Caleb pinned the words he wanted to mumble behind cold lips and followed. Ridiculous curiosity. Why did Thomas have to phrase it like a question? He knew it'd be as easy as leading a bull by the ring. His irritation flared. He wanted his quiet life back. No headstrong women. No absent fathers. No interfering foremen.

He ducked his head as they entered the stable. It took a moment for his eyes to adjust to the darker interior. The warmth from the animals thawed his nose.

Thomas huffed a laugh and pointed. "Just as her father predicted."

There, with her arms crossed and resting on the stall's half door, Miss Beauregard talked to Arion as if they were old school chums. Caleb stalked forward. "What do you think you're doing!"

Miss Beauregard jumped, but so did Arion. He snorted and kicked, and frustration ripped through Caleb. His outburst could have harmed Miss Beauregard. Or Arion. But she shouldn't have been here. Why couldn't she see she was going to get herself seriously injured?

"Shh, Arion." Miss Beauregard turned a shoulder to Caleb. "Your master is just being a beast this morning. That doesn't mean we need to get angry at him. I suspect you and he aren't so dissimilar. All tough on the outside and doughy on the inside. Hmm?"

Doughy? Her words brought him up short. Coherent thought blew away on the chill breeze that swept through the stable. She didn't lecture him? Scold? Or even grow as equally irritated as he? Usually his gruffness served well to give him the space he craved. Yet she seemed to see right through that. Though soft was a word that had never applied to him.

Arion snorted again. And Miss Beauregard smiled. "Yes, not so dissimilar at all. You both could use with a little gentling to know you're safe and secure, then free you to ride on the wind. You'd like that, wouldn't you, Arion? You might just sprout wings like your namesake."

"I don't need gentling," Caleb growled, needing to fortify his battlements. This, this, *compassion* of hers would do him no good. "And neither does Arion. He's to be a stud horse. Not for a lady to ride to a picnic."

Miss Beauregard laughed. A sound that brought to mind the pansies that could bloom in the face of Montana Territory's icy spring.

"Ma'am? A letter from your father." Thomas stepped forward, breaking whatever spell Miss Beauregard attempted to weave. Good.

There was no place for her feminine wiles on his ranch. Time to send her back to Beauregard.

"Oh?" Confusion tugged her lips into a frown as she accepted the folded paper and began reading. He didn't like seeing that expression on her face, which made no sense whatsoever. Worse, the more she read, the deeper the frown grew.

"What is it?" Caleb demanded, barely keeping himself from snatching the letter from her hands.

"My father insists I stay here." She raised her gaze to his. Uncertainty and hurt swirled there. "He knows I will want to help Arion, and he thinks I'm safer here than with him now that everyone knows I'm … I'm … a girl."

"Give me that." He grabbed the letter. "How could you be safer here? I'm not the marrying kind and won't be party to ruining your reputation." And with Doran nearby, Beauregard was best off taking her far away from here. What was the man thinking!

"That's why he sent me with this, sir." Thomas held out a sealed envelope with Caleb's name on it. "He also made me swear that the missus and I would not only act as chaperones but take Miss Beauregard under our wing."

For the first time since he spotted her racing after Arion yesterday afternoon, Miss Beauregard seemed to shrink. She hugged her arms around her stomach and inched closer to Arion's stall door. Away from Caleb and Thomas. He tore open the letter, wishing her father was here so he could give him a few choice words.

Mr. Orson, I've been on this mountain for a long time. I know the man who gave you the land on which you built your ranch and so know what he thinks of you. On that esteem, I am entrusting my daughter. Nomadic life is no existence for her. And now that she has caught Doran's eye, she needs you to guard her. Do this, not for me or her, but because of the man Ahanu believes you to be.

Caleb reread Beauregard's letter, emotion clogging his throat at Ahanu's name. The old Blackfoot warrior had taken Caleb in during those dark days just after the war. But Ahanu's health failed, and he, like many of his people, risked losing the land he'd settled after the 1855 treaty. So he and several others had given Caleb their land under the promise to protect and care for it and all those who came to live on it.

He refolded the letter and met Miss Beauregard's soft brown eyes. "Welcome to Crooked Tooth Ranch, Miss Beauregard. You're welcome to stay as long as you'd like."

Chapter Four

Sallie leaned low over Gunpowder's neck, giving him his head and letting him tear across the open expanse east of Crooked Tooth Ranch. She'd never been away from Papa for more than a day, and she couldn't reconcile his leaving her here without even a proper goodbye.

And so, over the past eleven days, she mainly kept to herself because she didn't feel like herself. Mr. and Mrs. Thomas, especially Mrs. Thomas, tried to welcome her. The older lady was a phenomenal cook. But Sallie couldn't dredge up a conversation except with the horses.

The icy wind whipped through her hair, tearing it from its braid as Gunpowder's hooves beat the slushy snow. Winter refused to give up easily, the chill air stealing her breath while the sun warmed her. Just now, she liked the battle it caused. It matched the tumult that had been building.

Mr. Orson watched her work with Arion, but always from a distance. In fact, he hadn't spoken to her since his official welcome to the ranch. It irked her, his standoffish ways. Yes, he let her work with Arion, but it felt more like he grudgingly allowed it than requested it because she knew horses. Infuriating man.

Arion, however, was her bright spot besides her daily rides on Gunpowder. She patted Gunpowder's neck and urged him to slow to a canter. After Arion's escape, the black fought anyone who dared tie his lead rope. She guessed he expected more wood to crash like it had the day he ran away. Poor horse.

However, as long as they were in the corral, Arion would let her—and only her—rub him down. Of course, Mr. Orson, Mr. Thomas, or one of the ranch hands was always nearby as if they worried the stallion would trample her underfoot. Did they think her a fool? She respected the power rippling under the muscles of such a steed. If she didn't, then there would be cause to worry. But fear had no place in building trust.

She pressed her left heel into Gunpowder's flank, turning him so the rising sun would be at their back, and taking stock of her surroundings. Whoops. They'd gone much farther than she intended. Several miles from the ranch, if she calculated correctly. Perhaps a touch foolish.

"Sorry ol' boy." She patted his neck and slowed Gunpowder to a trot, then a walk.

Gunpowder bobbed his head. He loved to run, but she shouldn't have run him so hard for so long.

"Let's take our time getting back, then I promise you a good rubdown and extra oats. Do you like that idea?"

A snort was Gunpowder's answer. Sallie smiled. This is what she'd needed. An escape. The untamed wilderness to surround her. To let her spirit fly free.

Oh that I had wings like a dove! for then would I fly away, and be at rest ... then would I wander far off, and remain in the wilderness.

The Psalmist's wish from Psalm 55 whispered on the breeze. Would that she could remain in the wilderness. She could befriend the animals. They never judged her or ogled her or felt sorry for her. They offered her mutual respect.

Oh, but many would also be slowly waking this time of year. Hungry and cranky from a winter's sleep. Wisdom said to give them time to fill their bellies. Animals—and people—were always more agreeable on a full stomach. Which didn't explain Mr. Orson's surliness. Mrs. Thomas was a fine cook.

Her stomach gurgled. Had she truly gone so far that it was nearing the noon meal? She glanced at the sun to guage the time. Sure enough. Would anyone at Crooked Tooth Ranch note her absence? Did she wish them to?

A prickle raised the hair on the back of her neck. She wasn't alone, though she could see no movement. She urged Gunpowder to pick up his pace. Eagles could soar so high they were out of sight, but she didn't think that was what watched her. The feeling came from the north. An animal? A human? She saw no mark on the landscape, so an animal made more sense. In which case, it could be a cougar or wolf. Dangerous.

Gunpowder shifted to the side with a snort, obviously sensing her unease. Or did he sense the eyes on them, too? Instinct urged her to run, and she felt Gunpowder's muscles tightening to do just that. But wisdom told her to keep a steady pace. Predators chased prey, and if they ran, that's what they'd become.

She spotted a rock outcropping ahead. A good place to hide, so she turned Gunpowder toward it. Her horse chuffed, a hitch in his step. She held him steady.

"Easy, ol' boy." The quiver in her voice would do the horse no good.

Again, she scanned the area to the north and this time she caught movement. A shadow, low to the ground, slinking through the grass. A cougar, no doubt. Hungry, thinking it had come upon a tired, lone horse separated from its herd. A burst of speed, a pounce, and she or Gunpowder would be the big cat's meal.

Unless she could make the big cat rethink his perspective.

The rock outcropping drew closer, but the cougar even moreso. Sallie's heart pounded as she eyed the rifle in the saddle boot. She never went anywhere without it, and if it came down to Gunpowder or the cat, she'd choose Gunpowder. But she hated the thought of harming the animal. Sure, Papa was a trapper, but he respected the animals he caught and thanked them and God for the provision their sacrifice cost. The meat he preserved and sold to hungry souls. The pelts he turned into clothing. Each part of a critter was put to use, as the Blackfeet had taught him.

But the hesitation cost her. She knew it the next instant. The cat hissed. Gunpowder squealed, bucked, and Sallie's lack of attention sent her flying off Gunpowder's back.

She hit the ground with a thud that reverberated through her body, and before she could blink, Gunpowder—along with her water and weapon—took off toward the mountains. Would he go to the ranch or go home? Would the cat chase after him or see her as easy prey? She grimaced as she shifted, readying to act depending on what the cat decided.

The cougar took one step as if to follow the running horse before its gaze caught on Sallie. She knew in that instant the cat would come for her. She was weak, slow, easily caught. Even if she reached the outcropping, there was no protection for her there. She'd made an error in calculation, let her emotion drive her to risk too much. And now it would cost her life.

Caleb halted just inside the barn doorway and blinked. Did he really just see one of his cowhands strike a horse after it bit him? Considering the curse-laced words coming from Erman, yes, yes he did.

"What do you think you're doing?" Caleb yanked the middle-aged man away from the horse by the collar of his coat. "That is not how you treat an animal."

Erman smacked Caleb away. "It's my horse. I can do whatever I want."

"Not on my ranch." Caleb pointed toward the door. He had no time for the mistreatment of animals. "You're fired."

The man spat ugly words through thick lips. How had the man hidden his true nature the past year? He'd ask Thomas about it. After they removed the man from the premises. He almost offered to buy the horse, but the man would just buy another. It was why Caleb had kept Arion. Someone had to protect these horses from men who would abuse them. These magnificent creatures didn't deserve to be mistreated.

Sallie would agree with him. Hopefully, she hadn't witnessed this. Irritation fanned his anger—she occupied too much of his mind—and he reiterated his command for Erman to leave at a roar.

Erman scrambled to obey, and ten minutes later, the cowhand and his poor horse were sent on their way. However, Sallie hadn't appeared, which was unusual. He might not like having such a sense of her, but at least it gave him the awareness needed to protect her as her father requested.

Caleb returned to the barn in search of Sallie. Instead, he ran into Thomas, who explained she'd left on a ride.

"What do you mean *she left*?" Caleb growled at Thomas.

Thomas had the decency to look guilty. "She usually takes Gunpowder for a ride in the mornings. I didn't think much of it until I realized they hadn't returned yet."

"Why wasn't I made aware of this?" He stalked toward Duke's stall. In the past eleven days, how had he not noticed she left the ranch? Did she choose mornings because it was the time of day he locked himself in his library and demanded not to be disturbed? "She should never have been allowed to go out without an escort."

Thomas dogged him, ignoring the horses that reached their noses over the half door of their respective stalls. "You know, if you said even a word to her, maybe she wouldn't feel the need to escape you."

"Escape me? So this is *my* fault?" He jerked the bridle from the nail on which it hung, knew he needed to calm down before opening Duke's stall, but couldn't manage it quite yet.

He stared down his foreman. The horse might be battle-tested, but Caleb wouldn't subject him to his master's frustration. Thomas probably didn't even deserve it, though at this moment, Caleb wasn't so sure.

"I thought she was happy." His volume rose. "She had the horses. I let her get in the corral with Arion. Against my better judgment, mind you."

"And so you've missed how her smile has dimmed over the last week." Thomas folded his arms. "She's become a shadow of the woman I saw bring Arion home ten days ago."

Eleven days. Not that Caleb had been counting.

"From the first night when she could hardly stop chattering," Thomas went on, undeterred, "to barely saying *thank-you* to the missus for breakfast. She picks at her food, too. And my wife is an excellent cook."

She was, no doubt about it. Mrs. Thomas would bring him tea and sweet bread before he locked himself in his library each morning. After his nightly battle with sleep, the morning hours were the only time his mind allowed him to rest. And the thought was enough to allow him a deep breath, for understanding and compassion to break through his anger. Which, in turn, calmed him enough to be able to lead Duke from his stall and tether his lead to the hitching post outside.

"I'll go search for her." Caleb fit the bridle in Duke's mouth. "Do you know which direction she usually goes? Or better, which way she went this morning?"

"Aye. She always goes east, toward the flatlands. I believe she likes to gallop." The smile that tugged at Thomas's mouth raised Caleb's brow.

He settled the blanket, then the saddle over Duke's back. "Why is that amusing?"

"She likes wild things. Untamed things." The amusement moved to the man's eyes. "If you gave her half a chance, I think she'd like you, too."

"Hogwash." Caleb tightened the saddle girth. Yet, the thought of a woman liking him for who he was, not just despite his rough edges, but because of them ... an odd feeling took root in his chest. It spurred him on so that in no time, he was galloping along the path he hoped would bring him to her.

The noonday sun shone down overhead, just warm enough to melt the icy ground layer that built overnight. He searched the horizon and watched for signs of her along the way. Each minute seemed to tighten a rope around his chest. His blood pumped faster. She shouldn't be this far from the ranch. What if Doran had found her? Or a wild animal? Could she defend herself? Probably. But—

A black horse cantered toward him. Stirrups flapping. The rifle in the boot still in place. "Whoa, there. Where's your rider, Gunpowder?" The horse didn't slow.

Had he bucked her off? Maybe, but that surely wasn't the complete story. No way could a horsewoman like Sallie Beauregard simply fall off a horse without cause. He'd watched her with Arion these past ten—eleven—days. She knew how to manage an unruly horse, a scared horse, a temperamental horse. And with her bond to Gunpowder, his riderless presence had to mean something bad had happened.

The snarl of a cougar answered his questions. He sent Duke into a gallop and pulled his pistol from his belt. Gunpowder continued his flight west, but the poor beast was on his own for the moment.

It took an instant to take in the scene Gunpowder had left. Sallie stood on a rocky rise, waving her arms and—of course—talking to the cougar. He could hear bits and pieces of her words. Her attempt to warn off the big cat. The cougar stalked the ground around her. Caleb fired two shots into the air. Both the cat and Sallie turned toward him.

"Yah! Yah!" He shouted, firing two more shots. The cougar growled, then bounded away. Caleb holstered his pistol with a sigh of relief.

"Thank you." Sallie sank to the rocks, leaving her pale face at eye level when he brought Duke close. She raised shaky fingers to brush a stray strand of dark brown hair behind her ear. "I know better. I—"

"Don't." He waved off her explanations. They turned his exasperation at her into compassion, and he didn't like it. "Let's get you back to the ranch."

She nodded, but her shaky descent from the rock had him dismounting to offer her aid. Her hand slipped into his and sparked something he'd never felt before.

No, not entirely true. It was kin to the emotion that lodged in his chest when a baby animal fought for its life. When he rubbed a calf's chest, urging their little lungs to work as God intended. When he wrapped a colt in a blanket because its mother rejected it. When he bottle-fed a runt piglet because it wasn't strong enough to eat on its own.

But Sallie Beauregard was no fragile animal. So then, what was this new feeling?

"Thank you, Mr. Orson." She ducked her head as her feet touched the ground.

"Caleb." He growled, inexplicably tightening his grip on her. "Name's Caleb. Now get on the horse so we can find yours."

She moved so quickly he had no time to prepare for the gentle kiss she pressed to his cheek, above his beard. Then she was mounted on Duke, the reins in her hands. "Coming along, Mr. Orson? Or shall I leave you here?"

Crazy woman. He swung up behind her and reached around her narrow waist for the reins. She flicked her wrists to keep him from taking them, and he had no choice but to wrap his arms around her—and hold on for dear life—as Duke sprang forward. Her laugh splashed from her like a waterfall into a clear pool. Refreshing and reflecting all the colors of a rainbow.

Never had he met anyone quite like Sallie Beauregard. And he found he liked her way more than a broken man like himself had any right to do.

Chapter Five

The following day, Sallie forwent her usual ride. To focus on Arion, she tried to tell herself, but she knew better. Yesterday had shaken her more than she cared to admit.

She let Arion out of his stall and directed him into the attached corral, then into the next. This second corral was slightly smaller, which suited her purposes. She'd brought Arion here each day since they met.

Mist trailed along the ground, reflecting the rising sun. Her breath puffed in white plumes. Sallie clucked her tongue, and Arion snorted, but he continued to trot along the fence as he had since she began this routine. His muscles rippled as they warmed with action. He snorted again. This time, he slowed.

Whether it was by instinct, God's whisper, or something else, Sallie couldn't explain her innate *knowing* of that moment when a horse was ready to connect with her. The way Arion bobbed his head as he walked made her keep her eyes on him. She sensed it would happen today.

He slowed even more, then set his nose to the ground. Smiling, she turned her back to him.

One. Two. Thr—

A velvety nose appeared over her left shoulder. She slowly raised her hand to touch his coarse coat. "Good boy."

Taking care to keep her breathing even, she turned until she could press her right cheek to Arion's. With purposeful movement, she trailed her fingers up his forelock to his ears, then stepped forward to slide her hands down his neck. Shifting to the side, she ran her hand down his leg, feeling for injury or inflammation. All appeared sound. She tapped his knee and he lifted his hoof. It could use a better cleaning than he'd allowed her to do thus far.

"Good boy." She patted his shoulder. "Go on."

Arion wagged his head. Sallie clucked her tongue, and the horse trotted off toward the fence. Eventually, she was able to check all four legs and hooves. Tomorrow, she'd bring out the hoof pick and brushes to re-introduce those tools and remind him that they helped, even if they'd had to be forced on him for the last little while.

Before she pushed him past his limit, she rubbed him down and secured him in his cleaned stall with fresh water in his half-barrel and a cup of oats in his feed. She stopped in the stable doorway and closed her eyes against the semi-warm sun. Not even noon and the day felt like victory.

"Where did you learn to work with horses?"

Sallie startled at the deep voice beside her.

Caleb Orsen pushed off the stable wall, large yet lithe, like the cougar she met yesterday. "I thought you stopped because you saw me."

Had he been waiting for her here? Suddenly, not quite sure what to do with her hands, she stuffed them into the wide pockets of her coat. That didn't seem right, though. Why this flustering feeling? It hadn't been that way with Mr. Orson until yesterday. Until he scared the cougar away, and she kissed his cheek. She'd just been so grateful.

"Well?" Mr. Orson scowled at her. "Are you going to answer?"

What was the question? Oh, right, horses. No, not horses, exactly. Her ability to work with the animals. She bristled. "Why shouldn't I be able to work with horses?"

Mr. Orson narrowed his eyes, causing deep groves to form on his weathered face. The man wasn't old—only a few years her senior, she'd guess—but his face made him appear ancient. Whatever this man had faced in his past it left him scarred inside. And those inner wounds aged him.

She sighed. If he were a horse, she'd know exactly how to ease his pain. Then again, even though he was a man, perhaps she could try—should try—to help him.

"Walk with me?" The words were out before she could check her idea with a prayer. *Lord, is this what I'm supposed to do?*

"What do you mean?" Wariness had him stepping away just as Arion had done that first day in the corral.

Whatever flustered feeling that had pinned her tongue a few moments ago washed away. Horses needed to feel safe, respected, and welcomed into a herd. Perhaps this man wasn't all that different.

She raised a brow and offered a slight smile. "If you want an answer to your question, walk with me." Then, she started off toward an unused pasture.

A glance over her shoulder a moment later showed Mr. Orson shaking his head as he followed her. She faced forward before he could see her grin.

Yes, Caleb Orson was just like the magnificent beasts she loved to bring from fear to peace.

·❤·❤·❤·❤·❤·

Infuriating woman.

Caleb stomped after Sallie. He'd been merely acting on that odd feeling she caused in him yesterday. Now, she demanded a promenade? As if they were in Boston or New York? Did she think him a wealthy gentleman caller? He'd show her he wasn't anything like the polished dandies back east. He used to be one. Before the war. Before he escaped to live in the wilderness. Where wild nature fit the wild inside.

Clumps of icy-crusted snow dotted the pasture. They'd move the horses here once the grass returned. Ahead, Sallie stopped and crouched. Caleb slowed his steps, curiosity calming his ire.

"For, lo, the winter is past, the rain is over and gone," her voice whispered like the first warm breath of spring, "the flowers appear on the earth; the time of the singing of birds is come."

"A poem?" He leaned over her shoulder, spotted the clump of purple violas that rose out of the cold ground.

A red tint covered her cheeks and she kept her gaze averted. "Song of Solomon, actually. So, yes, a poem."

A young, unmarried woman reading such? It may be the Bible, but … "About that walk?" He held out a hand to aid her rise.

She slipped her fingers in his, and just like yesterday, that *something* punctured his chest. He kept hold of her, urging her close to his side so he could wrap her hand around his arm—a gentleman escorting a lady.

As if.

"Do you think other places are as beautiful as Montana Territory?" she asked. Not only did she not shy away from him, she seemed to lean into his arm. "I can't imagine a place that doesn't have meadows and mountains. Or a sky that seems to encompass the heavens."

"I suppose that's why I stayed." He'd never considered it before. Just knew he belonged here. A cool breeze brushed his beard.

"Before here, where did you call home?" Sallie's gaze wandered the horizon as if her question referred to the weather, not to the canyon in his soul.

He swallowed. "Illinois." And he probably still had extended family there. Maybe. Not that he planned to ever return. He wasn't the wide-eyed lad who left to join the Union army when the war began.

Sallie hummed. "I don't imagine you took a straight line from Illinois to Montana Territory."

A humorless laugh jumped from his throat. It had been anything but a straight line. A road through horrors he wished he could forget. She brought her free hand to his arm, as if to hug his biceps. Or hug him?

"Winter is the only time Papa and I stay in the same place. We have a little cabin in the mountains. Otherwise, we follow the animals." She spoke lightly, but he would be a fool to miss the pain underlying her words. If she hadn't chased after Arion, she'd be following her father right now, tracking the animals for meat and fur to feed and clothe others.

He coughed as if gravel stuck in his throat. And perhaps it did, so unaccustomed to asking personal questions as he was. "Do you like moving around like that?"

"Do I like it?" She tilted her head. "I don't believe I've ever considered that question before. It's always been what we did. I'll admit, I've always wished we could go farther, but we've never left Montana Territory as far as I know. So I go places in my books. But I'm not sure any place could be as beautiful as this."

Funny. He'd had the same thought when he first came upon the mountains. Feverish from a seeping wound. Ready to die. He'd looked up at majestic beauty and prayed. "Huh." The memory brought him to a halt. That's when Ahanu had found him.

"What?" She looked up at him, attentive, patient. Beautiful. "You can tell me."

He shook his head. He wouldn't burden her with his pain. It had no place in her sunshine. "You have yet to answer my original question. Where did you learn to work with horses?"

She studied him for a moment, then tugged him back into motion. "All right, Mr. Orson."

"Caleb." He wasn't sure why he insisted. It just seemed ... right.

"All right, *Caleb*. I take it you'll call me Sal, then?"

No. Not Sal. Sal was the trapper's kid. "The horses. *Sallie*."

"The horses." Did she tighten her hold on his arm? "It's a simple story, really. Long days on the trail with just my papa for company meant I had to find someone to talk to. My horse made the most sense. We were always together, whether following Papa or camped for the night. My first horse was an old mare. Slow. Gentle. Perfect for a little girl. She was my best friend."

Caleb worked his jaw, doing his best to keep from showing a reaction to her story. How lonely her childhood must have been. It echoed something inside him that he refused to acknowledge. "So you trained her?"

"She trained me." Her waterfall laugh. "So when I stumbled on Gunpowder, I knew exactly what to do."

"Stumbled on?"

"Mmhm. Sad story, his. Gunpowder's owner died in his cabin and so Gunpowder had no one to care for him. We found him trapped in his stall, having drank all his water and eaten all his food. He didn't trust a soul, but as I doctored him back to health, he began to twitch his ears at my voice."

Caleb barely held in a snort. Not at the story, at himself. The last couple days, *he* had been listening more intently for Sallie's voice. It's why he'd been outside the stable today when she emerged.

"Fortunately, we were on the trail, so I could heal his physical wounds before addressing his inner ones. No need for stalls in the wilderness. He wasn't fond of being hobbled, but liked being corralled much, much less."

Caleb's heart rate kicked up. It was just a story about a horse. Not him. Even if he could identify with how the horse felt.

"Eventually, Gunpowder let me brush him, and soon he followed me without a lead. I knew I had made progress. But winter was setting in, so we returned to the cabin. I had to get him to trust a stall again, or he'd die of exposure on our mountain." Sallie adjusted her grip on his arm. "First, my mare and I got him into the corral. That went easier than I expected, but food, water, and company eased him. Getting Gunpowder into the barn was a different story entirely. Each day, I inched his food closer to the door to the barn until I set it just inside. And none too soon. The first snow fell that night. But Gunpowder still wouldn't enter the barn, and with time not on my side—"

"Mr. Orson, sir?" The call stopped Sallie's story.

Usually, Caleb would appreciate being pulled away from a talkative female, but today, he wasn't keen on this interruption. He wanted to know how Sallie brought Gunpowder to trust her so thoroughly. Obviously the horse had no trouble with a stall now. "What is it, Anchorman?" He growled at the kid. Sallie's elbow jabbed his side.

"Bull got loose, sir." The kid moved his hand to his hat, then both to his belt, then flopped them to his sides. "Thomas sent me to get you."

Caleb suppressed a growl, not wanting to add to the kid's nervousness. Another loose animal. Just what he needed.

Sallie tugged on his arm. "Come on. I'll help."

"No." His bark came out low and deep. He shook his head. "Your father insisted I keep you safe. Facing down a bull is not safe."

She circled in front of him, hands on her hips. "Were you not listening to anything I just said? I spent my childhood talking to animals. And yes, I know how that makes me sound. But it works." A becoming blush brushed her cheeks even while she raised her chin.

She was right, of course. Caleb pinned his lips together to keep the corners from rising. "Fine. I'll let you help if you promise to finish your story. I want to know how you got Gunpowder into the barn."

Her mouth tilted into a teasing smile, and she took two steps backward, a twinkle in her eye. "It's a deal, Mr. Orson." Then she spun and urged Anchorman into a quick walk beside her. Rushing into danger, hurrying to the rescue. Not willing to let an animal face anything but safety if she could help it.

He watched her for a moment before following, his long legs gaining ground. If Sallie managed to heal her traumatized horse, was there hope she could heal him, too?

Chapter Six

Sallie woke with a cold nose and cold ears. Two blinks cleared her eyes, and she realized why. Snow piled against the glass of her little window. She burrowed deeper under the covers. *Dear Lord, keep Papa warm.* Then she tossed back the quilt and faced the day.

When she emerged from her room, the little house was quiet. Mrs. Thomas must already be preparing the cowhands' breakfast at the mess hall. Usually, Sallie walked over with the older lady to lend a hand, which meant that either Mrs. Thomas had left early or Sallie had overslept. And she never saw Mr. Thomas in the mornings since he was first out to get chores begun.

Sallie donned long johns under her buckskin pants. It had been three days since her walk with Mr. Orson—Caleb. She hadn't sought him out or shared more of Gunpowder's story like he made her promise. She didn't aspire to be forward, or even appear forward, especially after her impromptu kiss.

Making quick work of sliding on her gloves, she glanced down at her buckskin coat and moccasin boots. A pang caused her eyes to close. In the quietest moments, a longing whispered. A desire for home and hearth and a family of her own. A man who loved her, who would swing her around their tiny kitchen in a mountain dance. Her skirts sweeping the dusty floor where little ones played with hand-carved toys. Since that walk in the meadow with Caleb, the whisper was becoming a murmur.

She stuffed her hat over her hair and stomped out the door, the nagging loneliness chasing after her.

"Clear the stable!" Caleb's shout punctured the falling snow. Or was that the crack of wood?

Sallie ran for the low structure along with a dozen other cowhands. Ice hung from the edges of the roof, hinting at the problem. Heavy, wet snow had piled onto the slush that had been thawing and freezing the past few days, and now it threatened to cave in the roof.

She blinked against the dark interior of the stable. The men worked quickly, efficiently, moving horses into the attached corral. Caleb himself led Gunpowder. Assured her horse was safe, she wove her way to Arion's stall. The poor horse kicked and snorted against his pen. There was no time to put him at ease before they had to get him out, meaning she needed a hood. Cover the horse's eyes against the commotion.

"What are you doing in here?" Caleb's growl preceded him. He spun her around to face him, large hands gripping her shoulders. Soot and debris covered him, a rope hung over his shoulder, and his eyes sparked like flames. "Get out. Now."

"Get me a lariat." She stared him down. She'd need the lasso if the horse escaped the corral. "I leave with Arion."

He must have read her determination in her eyes because he only huffed as he slapped his rope into her hand. Then she opened the stall door.

Arion bucked, slapping his back hooves against the rear of the stall. Then he bolted. She used the stall door to direct him toward the rear of the barn, and he tore down the aisle. She raced after the terrified horse, knowing in this state, Arion could harm himself, another horse, or a human. And heaven forbid it if he attempted to jump the corral fence.

Another crack and Caleb's arm circled her waist. Like a sack of feed, he tossed her from the barn just as snow, wood, and debris tumbled into the center of the stable behind them.

"Foolish woman." He yanked her to her feet, glaring at her. "You could have been killed."

She jerked from his hold. "See to your men, Mr. Olson." Then she spun away, ignoring the angry muttering behind her. She whistled for Gunpowder. Where had Arion gone?

Arion had escaped into the empty corral beyond the one attached to the barn. Good. She could manage him there. Gunpowder trotted close, but just before she led him to the fence so she could mount bareback, Caleb's hand pressed her shoulder.

"Be careful." He huffed into her ear, then created a stirrup with his fingers and propelled her onto Gunpowder's back.

She hooked his lariat over her shoulder as she met his gaze. She could see both pain and concern swirling in his eyes. He was like a horse who lashed out because of its fear, and it made her hurt for him.

He raised his massive hand until it hovered over her knee. Chaos swirled around them, urgency snapped like lightning, yet he reached for her. She met him there, slipping her small hand, palm up, under his. He gripped her fingers, closed his eyes, then ran back into the collapsing barn.

Tucking the moment away, Sallie urged Gunpowder to follow Arion into the other corral. A cowhand closed the gate behind her. Arion ran along the fence line, and she brought Gunpowder alongside him. The terrified horse bucked, but she didn't back off. Round and round they went as she let Arion feel Gunpowder's steady nerves. Free of the residual memories of his own trauma, her horse could show Arion he had nothing more to fear.

Finally, Arion looked at her and met her eyes. She backed off. "That's it, ol' boy," she murmured.

Giving him a moment, she returned Gunpowder to his side.

They repeated this series of events several more times until Arion finally slowed to a walk. Then she directed Gunpowder to the center of the corral. Arion continued walking along the fence for another half turn. Sallie waited. Only ambient noise filtered around them, so the cowhands must have gone, though she couldn't remember them leaving. Snow fell gently and she looked for the telltale glow of the sun behind the dark clouds. How long had she been at this?

Before she conjured an answer, Arion stepped beside her and Gunpowder.

"Hey, ol' boy. Feeling better now?"

The horse nosed her leg, and she smiled.

Movement out of the corner of her eye drew her attention. Caleb stood outside the corral, one boot on the bottom rail, arms resting on the top one. He met her gaze, jaw set. Then he turned and walked away.

Caleb couldn't breathe. He stalked away from the corral, unwilling to let Sallie experience his temper.

He'd slipped up enough in that regard. She didn't deserve his surliness. No one did. But her especially. And he wasn't mad at her. No, his anger was directed squarely at himself because she could have been killed, and what did he do? Let her ride bareback in a corral with a crazed horse. No, not just let. He helped! When he should have stopped her.

He kicked at a slushy pile of snow along the outside of the pasture fence, imagining the clod was his own backside.

"Caleb?" she called after him, question woven into how she said his name.

He clenched his fists against the memory of her touch and kept his pace. If she was determined, she could run to catch up. If not, then she'd leave him alone. He wanted the latter, but hoped for the former.

He hated how he craved her presence and found ways to be around her without realizing he'd done so. Weakness. It was what it was, and he could ill-afford it. No, *she* could ill-afford it. 'Twas dangerous for her to be near him. He'd only harm her.

Yet. Yet! He couldn't deny how she had calmed Arion today, managing a connection with the horse no one else had achieved. She kept the beast safe, too, and survived in one piece. Still. His chest ached at what could have happened. The pain of it lanced where his heart should have been. War had carved out his soul so that he was barely fit to care for the animals under his protection. If not for the promise Ahanu extracted for how to use his land, Caleb would have disappeared into the wilderness long ago.

He stomped an icy chunk under his boot. Shouldn't he be more concerned about the destroyed barn than the perfectly hale woman in his charge? Even as the thought entered his mind, he knew what Ahanu would say.

Caleb scrubbed his bearded face, shoulders heavy with the responsibility. Winter would keep its grip for several more weeks, and his horses needed shelter. He'd have to direct resources—men and money—to repair the roof at once. Which meant a trip into town with Thomas. He hated going into town.

"Caleb, slow down. Please." Sallie called again from about the same distance behind him, but her tone had changed. A plea he hadn't heard before. He spun. Caught her grimace before she hid it as she leaned against a fence post. Now, what had he done?

His long stride allowed him to reach her in an instant. "What's wrong?" Had he been mistaken about her being unharmed? And here he'd been storming off like a child.

She waved her hand in the air with a self-deprecating groan. "I'm fine. Just stumbled. Honest. I'll be right as rain in a minute, but I didn't want you to get too far ahead of me."

Stumbled? Because he was walking too fast. Ignoring her. Like an ogre. He ran his gaze over her, searching for evidence of the truth. Just how much pain was she hiding from him? No snow to indicate a fall. He forced himself to raise his eyes to hers, surprised to find no judgment there. "Are you sure?"

"That I'm fine? Or that I don't blame you? Or that I simply didn't want you to get too far ahead?" Then she left the fencepost to weave her arm around his like she had the other day. He made to protest, then realized she leaned on him. She had hurt her ankle worse than she would admit.

"You are hurt. I'll carry you to the main house. Mrs. Thomas will see to you."

She held him back with a hand to his chest and tilted her head to study him. What was she thinking? And why did it make him all itchy?

"Sallie." He put distance between them, causing her arm to leave his, then remembered her ankle. He cupped her elbow to steady her.

"I'm all wrong for you. I don't know why your father left you here. I ..."

She pressed her thin fingers against his mouth, stalling the words in his throat. Words he couldn't quite believe came from *his* mouth. How could he admit such a thing to her? And since when did he feel anything toward anyone? Especially something that implied the romantic?

A blush reddened her cheeks, and she snatched her hand away to hug herself. "I don't like when you put yourself down. Just because you don't think you're a good man doesn't make it true."

"How can you know that?" And why did the answer matter so much?

"Because you stopped when you realized I might be hurt. Because you are angry that I could have gotten hurt with the horses. Because ..." The blush in her cheeks turned to flaming red. "Because if I were ever so bold ... You know what, never mind."

She spun away, but she hissed when she stepped on her ankle. He snagged her arm to keep her from falling, even as his heart pounded when the implications of her words sank in. Not only what she thought of him and that she'd defended him, though that was enough to make him puff out his chest. But she implied more, just as he had.

He circled to face her. "Sallie, finish that sentence."

"No." She ducked her head away. She wasn't a brazen woman. Bold, yes. Stubborn, yes. But it had been her defense of him that lowered her guard enough that her wish nearly seeped through. A wish to … get to know him? Care about him? Maybe kiss him?

He needed to banish that thought from his mind. He couldn't kiss her. Though, right now, dredging up the reasons he couldn't felt like hauling mud. He swung his head like one of his massive bulls. "You can't like me, Sallie. I'm not good enough for you."

Her chin shot up, and she pierced him with blazing eyes. "And that's my point. You are good. You're protecting me. Don't you see?" She jabbed a finger into his chest.

He pinned her hand to his chest to keep her from poking him. "Your father asked me to protect you. I won't compromise you. I won't betray the trust he placed in me."

"You are not Doran." So emphatic was she that she flung her free arm out, nearly losing her balance when she stepped back on her injured foot. He caught her about the waist, but it didn't slow her down. "Doran thinks only of himself and how he can use people, especially women. He'd turn me into a trophy. I'm a prize to purchase. Nothing more. That is not you. Do you hear me?"

His back bent against the truth she didn't see. "I have a darkness in me, Sallie. It's what war does to a man. I've seen too much. I've killed my fellow human beings. And you? You're all that is good and beautiful. I would only drag you down."

Her beautiful eyes turned to liquid, breaking his pounding heart. "I'm not good or beautiful, Caleb. Look at me, dressing like a boy to hide my womanhood."

He scoffed, but she silenced him with a shake of her head.

"You talk of darkness, Mr. Orson. Let me tell you about loneliness. When the stars above feel like your closest friends. When the night presses in like it will never end. When I'm left on a ranch I've never visited with people I've never met. Alone. Deserted. Bereft. Without mother, father, friend." She motioned toward the cows huddled nearby. "Left to talk to animals because there is no other living thing with whom to speak. To escape into the pages of a book in order to see the world beyond the mountains I love."

He cupped her cheek, her pain echoing his own. "Then how is it you can reach horses?" *Reach me?*

She took a moment to fill her lungs, then let the air out in a slow release that left peace on her features. "I have to remember that I am not actually alone. That God will never leave me. That no matter the danger, the hardship, the darkness, God is there. Will always be there. That He's never more than a breath away."

He wanted to wrap his arms around her, comfort her, wanting that peace, that surety for himself. "Is that what we feel when we're around you? The horses. Me. Is that the goodness, the beauty that draws us?"

Pink tinged her cheeks as the corners of her mouth tipped up. "I pray so, Caleb. I truly do."

He stared at the mountains beyond her, her words reaching those dark places inside. How could she see God in the darkness? Maybe she could show him before he returned her to her father and they left him to his self-imposed solitude.

Then he wrapped one arm around her waist, the other under her knees, and carried her to his house.

Chapter Seven

"Caleb!" Sallie squealed as he lifted her in his arms, leaving her no choice except to rest against his massive chest. She wanted to relax, to sink into the safety of this place, but that would be highly improper. "Caleb, please put me down."

He shook his head and didn't stop his tromping through the slushy snow. "I'm taking you to Mrs. Thomas. You are injured. I'd do this for a calf, and I can do this for you."

"But I'm not a calf." The words escaped on a laugh at the comparison until she pictured him carrying such a gangly baby animal, and her insides melted into a puddle at the image. This giant of a man with a helpless creature in his arms.

"No, you aren't, but until I get you to the house, you are." His throat bobbed. "I can't watch you get hurt, Sallie."

Yes, her ankle throbbed, but she knew he spoke of her heart. She rested her head on his shoulder and placed her hand over the beating organ in his chest. What had he seen, been forced to do, that he felt so unlovable?

She knew, in her head, the horrors of war, but she'd never witnessed another human die. Animal, yes, but not human. Her father had sent her to the barn before her mother breathed her last, and he never let her see Gunpowder's previous owner. How much worse to be the instrument that took the life of another?

Tears burned her eyes. "I'm sorry, Caleb, for all you've had to experience."

His step stumbled, but he marched onward. Silent, focused on his destination. Past the destroyed barn, Arion in the corral, the bunkhouse ... until he stomped up the porch steps leading to the main house. A building she'd never stepped foot in before. She shivered at the thought of entering, even though she knew Caleb was an honorable man.

"Don't worry." His voice was gruff as he maneuvered inside without bumping her. "I'll deliver you into Mrs. Thomas's capable hands, then make myself seen outside so no one will question your reputation."

She remained silent, taking in this place where he lived. So much wood ... the floors, the walls ... logs hewn into a home. He stopped before the first set of double doors on the right, and the hesitation brought her head up from his shoulder.

"What's in there?" She sensed it was important to him, and it wasn't the kitchen where she would have expected to find Mrs. Thomas.

His chest expanded in a deep breath. "It's my ... library." The way his jaw flexed, she suspected the room meant much more.

However, she latched onto the one thing she hadn't expected to have in common with him. "You have books?"

"See for yourself." He, again, managed to open a door without jostling her and carried her inside.

She gasped. The room was, indeed, filled with books. Shelves and shelves of books. Two massive windows overlooked the yard and allowed light into the dark room. A fireplace with glowing coals took up the far wall and a large wooden desk was tucked nearby, as was a couch and a large chair. But on every open wall space stood a bookcase, and each bookcase was filled.

"You have so many." She wiggled, wanting him to set her on her feet so she could explore.

He tightened his hold on her and marched to the couch. "You can look later. I'll get Mrs. Thomas to see to your foot."

Curiosity driving her, she sat up as soon as he placed her on the cushions. Except he knelt and gently pressed her shoulder until she lay back again.

"Please, Sallie. It's my fault you were hurt. Let me do this for you." His quiet plea brought her attention away from the tomes lining the walls to the book that was Caleb Orson. Anguish contorted his weathered features.

"Not your fault." How could she get him to understand? "You do not need to serve penance, Caleb."

He shook his head and opened his mouth to no doubt protest. Sallie rested her palm against his scratchy beard, effectively trapping his words unsaid. Telling him her ankle was barely a twinge would not help. He took responsibility for something he didn't cause merely because she chose to follow him.

"Oh, Caleb." She stared into his eyes, willing for him to hear her. "You did not hurt me."

He flinched, but his grimace relaxed when she didn't back down. His gaze did not, however. He studied her as Arion did, fear and faith battling for control. Would he see her sincerity? That this was but an accident? That she alluded to a deeper meaning?

She did not blame a horse for lashing out in pain or fear. Neither did she blame him. He was not like Doran, who used his power and arrogance to get his way. Pain or fear may have turned some people into men like Doran, but there inlay the crux of the matter and what made a person different from the equine beasts she loved. Caleb's pain and fear humbled him, and instead of nursing his anger into a threat, he protected others from the darkness within.

Compassion washed over her like an avalanche. She rubbed her thumb along his cheekbone, and he closed his eyes. Like a whisper, the hope she wished to impart came to her mind in the form of a verse from First John. "You are of God, Caleb Orson, and have overcome them: because greater is he that is in you, than ..."

Her words trailed off as he leaned forward, his arm bracing against the back of the couch. Though he did not touch her, he hemmed her in. Anyone else, and she'd scramble to escape. Yet, just now, she didn't move.

She sensed a battle raging inside him, and she let it. Like with Arion, forced trust was no trust at all. It must be a choice.

Her heart beat against her ribs and her arm ached from holding her hand against his cheek, but still, she dare not move. *Lord, you say "there is no fear in love; but perfect love casteth out fear: because fear hath torment." If ever there was a man in torment who needs to feel Your love for him, it is this man.*

And then he leaned closer, and her prayer dissolved. His breath—and the scent of coffee—brushed her face. His beard tickled her chin as his lips neared hers. She'd never been kissed before. Had never been this close to a man before. But if there was ever a moment, a first, a—

A growl rumbled from his throat, and he bounded to his feet. Before she could gather her wits, he was gone.

· ♥ · ♥ · ♥ · ♥ · ♥ ·

He'd nearly kissed her.

Caleb stormed out of the house, having informed Mrs. Thomas of her latest patient. Why had he thought bringing Sallie into his house was a wise idea? He could have sent someone for Mrs. Thomas. *He* could have gone for Mrs. Thomas, *after* he deposited Sallie in the sick room.

"Boss?"

The title didn't clear the fog of self-recrimination from his eyes, and he batted the cowhand away with a snap of words. "Talk to Thomas."

How had he lost such control of himself that he nearly kissed this woman he'd promised to protect? Him? A beast, a broken man, the taker of lives, kissing a beautiful, innocent woman. The thought of the harm he could—perhaps had already caused!

He ripped a fallen board from where it blocked the way into the destroyed barn. If only he could rip himself for such a … a … *mistake*?

His chest ached in a way he hadn't felt since his first battle. A green soldier tossed into utter madness, forced to kill to save the friend at his side. Though it hadn't mattered in the end: the sun hadn't set before his friend had died in his arms.

Holding Sallie today, carrying her, had brought all that back to him. The torture, the memories. He tossed another cracked beam out of his way, demanding his muscles excise the feeling of her in his arms. How it felt to protect and succeed rather than fail.

Except he had failed.

Her touch had undone him. No, her words. What had she said? The words blurred in his mind, but one rose: overcome. Yes, he was overcome, but that wasn't what she meant. He recognized the words from the Bible. They were about God overcoming, not man.

Caleb tossed a broken stall door onto the floor, then lay another atop it. Where was that passage from? Five broken doors later, and it still hadn't come to him.

"Caleb Orson." Thomas's command halted his work. "You're a man of integrity, so what are you doing in here?"

Caleb's brows shot to his hairline. "What did you say?"

Thomas folded his arms, the sun casting a long shadow ahead of him. "You forbid the men from coming in here alone because it would be too dangerous, yet here you are."

He had said that because it was the truth. This recklessness of his was ... he groaned. "Do I have a death wish?"

Thomas jerked his head for Caleb to follow, and he did. Out into the sunlight and along the same path he'd taken to run away from Sallie. Did Thomas know? Probably. Not much could stay hidden in the wide open spaces. His pride pricked at the thought of his cowhands seeing the foreman rebuke the boss, but Caleb deserved it.

They stopped along the same fence where Caleb had lifted Sallie into his arms. Had it been less than an hour ago? Definitely less than two. Caleb leaned his back against the rail that kept the cows closer to the main barn this time of year.

Thomas faced him. "This death wish, as you call it, wouldn't be about the pretty miss who just hurt her ankle now, would it?"

Caleb sighed. How did he answer such a question?

"That sigh tells me more than words." Thomas chuckled. "You care about her."

He did. A lot.

"And you don't think you're good enough for her."

"Are you a mind reader?" The words shot out, and he opened his mouth to apologize, but Thomas held up his hand to stop him.

"I've known you since you came to this ranch, Caleb. The missus brought you back to health. Ahanu made us promise to look after you like the child we could never have." Thomas circled to face Caleb. "So, I tell you this with the love of a father."

Caleb nodded, welcoming yet fearing what Thomas would say. Surely, he was about to warn him to stay away from Sallie. Then, he could assure his foreman that had been his plan. That Sallie was safe from Caleb as much as she was from anyone who could harm her.

"Sallie Beauregard is a good woman," Thomas began.

"I know." Caleb kicked at a slushy clump of snow and braced for the reprimand that came next.

"I don't think you do." Thomas planted his hands on his belt. "A woman like Sallie is worth more than all the gold in these mountains."

Caleb came off the fence. "You don't think I know that?"

Thomas didn't budge. "She's the type of woman who will do a man good, not evil, for as long as she lives."

Being stabbed repeatedly hurt less—his hand strayed to his side—he would know. "Just say it already."

Thomas rolled his eyes. "Paraphrasing ain't doing you no good, so I'll just quote it for you. *The heart of her husband—*"

Caleb's eyes about bucked straight out of his head. "I'm not marrying her!"

"Ha! So you've thought about it." Thomas grinned like a fool. "She'd be good for you, Caleb. You trust her already."

Caleb shook his head. "That's not the point. Of course, she'd be good for me. Sallie is everything that's good and beautiful and innocent, which is exactly why I can't have anything more to do with her."

"You're willing to sacrifice for her. Live in loneliness. Give up her sunlight to give her what you think is a better life." Thomas yanked off his cowboy hat. "You're afraid you can't love her."

"Finally, you get it." Caleb flung out his arms, though his exasperation stuttered as the word *love* soaked in. Did he love Sallie? Surely not.

"I do get it, Caleb, which is why I want you to listen closely to what I'm about to say." Thomas's instruction was that of a general. "Ready?"

Caleb nodded, already off-kilter.

"Perfect love casts out fear, and we love because God first loved us." Thomas pinned him with a stare. *Love.* Again.

Like a lightning strike, Caleb realized that Thomas quoted from the same passage Sallie had. It sent him reeling and he took a physical step back, his boot slipping on a patch of ice.

Thomas advanced, finger jabbed into Caleb's chest. "Do you believe God loves you? Because that pretty young miss sure does. And I do, too."

Caleb regained his balance, but his jaw flopped open. Thomas jammed his hat on his head and stalked off. Caleb simply stared at the place where his foreman had stood, his world quaking beneath him.

When had love entered the equation?

Chapter Eight

Sallie slipped around the broken stable, headed toward the corral where Gunpowder and Arion had spent the night. Fortunately, the day had dawned warm and pleasant after yesterday's snow had caved in the roof. An April Fool's trick, for sure. Sallie knew snow could yet fall before spring took firm hold, knew it was what prompted Caleb and Mr. Thomas to ride into town this morning. So she would try not to hold it against them for not inviting her along.

The caged feeling urged her toward the corral though her stiff ankle slowed her. She needed a ride. To feel the wind on her face. To … She stopped at the fence. Arion snorted and tossed his head, then rose up and pounded his front feet on the ground. Gunpowder gave him a wide berth as he trotted over to Sallie.

"What's going on with him?" Sallie greeted Gunpowder with a pat to the neck. He nuzzled her, and she ran her other hand up his cheek, then down his forelock. "How's my boy this morning? Arion didn't bother you too much, did he?"

Gunpowder sniffed down her coat to her pocket.

"Ah, you know Mrs. Thomas gave me a carrot for you, hmm? She went up to the big house to make stew for supper." Sallie pulled out the carrot, broke it in two, and set half on the corral post for Gunpowder to eat and the other back in her pocket. She'd save it for Arion. "Mrs. Thomas warned me to keep out of the way today. I guess the cowhands take April Fools seriously. I never did understand the allure."

April Fools was a holiday that likely began by making fun of people who celebrated the wrong new year. Sallie huffed. Just because some people didn't know the calendar had changed from the Julian calendar to the Gregorian calendar was no reason to tease. And to perpetuate a celebration of making jokes at the expense of the gullible? Cruel.

"Shall we find out what has Arion all out of sorts?" She ducked between the fence rails instead of using the gate and her ankle protested the movement. The joint didn't hurt exactly, but a false move would reinjure it.

She walked slowly and Gunpowder followed with his head at her left shoulder. Arion skittered away as she approached. Sallie stopped in the center of the corral, Gunpowder beside her, and watched the other horse. The black stallion trotted along the fence, shaking his head. Agitation rippled over him.

"Alight, ol' boy." She waved her arms to keep him moving around the fence. "There you go."

She studied the horse, debating the best course. After the roof collapsed yesterday, a setback was expected, but she couldn't let Arion sink back too far. Deciding a buddy would be her ally today, she returned to the fence, commanded her ankle to stay strong, and scrambled up to sit on Gunpowder's bare back. Weaving her left hand into his mane, she urged him to trot alongside Arion. The stallion met her eye, so she backed off for a moment. Arion slowed, and she brought Gunpowder to his side again.

"Whatcha doing?" The loud voice broke the quiet morning. She jumped, causing Gunpowder to startle and pain to slice up her calf. Worse, Arion whinnied and kicked into a canter, her work undone.

She turned to the cowhand who acted so cluelessly, only for her words to die on her tongue when she realized the voice didn't belong to a cowhand but to Brendan Doran. Was that why Arion had been so testy? Doran rested a boot on a lower fence rung, arms crossed on a post. Similar to how Caleb had watched her yesterday, and yet Doran gave off a cocky air far different from her host.

"I assumed you'd be tired of Orson's company by now." Doran ran his leering gaze over her, making a violent streak rise, one she hadn't realized she had. "Surly man that he is, no wonder you keep company with horses. But never mind him, I know how to appreciate a beauty like you."

"I'm not interested, Mr. Doran," Sallie spoke through gritted teeth. Her fingers itched for a rope, a pistol even, something to make this man go away.

"Don't play the April Fool with me, Miss Beauregard." He ducked into the corral, sending her pulse skittering like Arion had done. Gunpowder stepped sideways. Arion huffed from behind her. "I know you would make me a perfect wife. And I mean to have you."

Oh, how she despised this so-called holiday. "I'm not interested, Mr. Doran. Please go away."

"What prospects do you have, Sal?" He advanced like the cougar from the other day. "I'm the best man around, and you know it."

Caleb couldn't rescue her this time—he was in town, or he would—which meant she needed to apply the same tactics she'd tried with the big cat. Make herself large and loud. Disabuse him of the notion she was weak prey. Sallie urged Gunpowder to a halt in front of Mr. Doran. His chest puffed, and self-importance lit his eyes. Never had she met a man, a person, who inspired such disdain and disquiet to fill her. She hated the feeling, hated the ugliness of it.

"Mr. Doran, I'll say it again: I am not interested." She met his gaze with a mountain of determination and raised herself straight on Gunpowder's back, the bite of pain in her ankle steeling her response. Would that she had stirrups so she could stand! "Now, please leave me alone before I call for reinforcements to make you leave Mr. Orson's property."

Red mottled his chiseled face, and he shook a finger toward her. "You'll regret your decision, Sal. Your beauty is too much to ignore. I'll be back for you when you realize your mistake. Then even Orson won't be able to stand in my way."

Cold snaked through Sallie as she watched Mr. Doran stalk away. What disaster had she put in motion by revealing her gender? If only her father hadn't deserted her to Caleb's care. Now, he was in the middle of this, too.

She glanced over at Arion. He trotted, then turned and tossed his head. Still agitated. And in her present state of mind, she'd only make it worse.

"Sorry, Gunpowder. We'll run tomorrow. You stay with Arion. I think it best I stick to my room today."

Maybe she'd see if Mrs. Thomas had a compress for her ankle, and ask whether she could choose a book from Caleb's collection. Anything to help speed the setting sun on this horrible day.

Caleb breathed easier as he and Thomas cantered onto the ranch mid-afternoon. Thomas still chuckled over the prank the miller had played on the owner of the sawmill. Something about a bag of grain filled with sawdust. Caleb didn't pay much mind.

Something had urged him to return to the ranch as quickly as possible. Or to have stayed this morning in the first place. It was the same intuition he'd get in battle, the one that had saved his hide too many times. The sense to duck only for a bullet to fly over his head. He'd have listened to it and stayed home had his horses not needed him to rebuild their shelter.

He searched the ranch for anything amiss. Saw nothing.

The new kid, Anchorman, took Duke's reins as they reached the corral. "I'll give him a good rubdown, sir."

Caleb nodded, then stopped the kid with a hand on the shoulder. "Anything out of the ordinary happen while we were gone?"

Thomas dismounted beside him.

"Yeah, actually." Anchorman tapped up the brim of his cowboy hat. "Doran stopped by to see Miss Beauregard."

"What!" That scoundrel must have seen Caleb in town and knew he could get to her. He scanned the yard again. If Doran hurt—

"She's fine, sir." Anchorman cast him that cheeky grin only a youth could muster, and it redirected Caleb's focus to the kid. "I kept my eye on him, and Miss Beauregard gave him the cold shoulder. Got her dander right up, though. Doran undid the work she'd done with the horses. Last I seen her, Mrs. Thomas let her into your library."

Relief swept through him, and Caleb slapped the kid on the back. He was making strides to fit in on the ranch. "Good work, Anchorman. Anticipating what is needed before you are asked will serve you well here at the Crooked Tooth." He gave Thomas a look that conveyed his foreman should take the youth more soundly under his wing. Kid had potential.

Anchorman reddened. "Thank you, sir. Miss Beauregard is a nice lady, and I know you fancy her, so I don't want nothing to happen to her."

Caleb laughed to keep his face from heating. "Just gotta learn to keep quiet before you say too much."

"Yeah, but I agree with the kid, boss." Thomas winked. "C'mon, Anchorman. I got a job for you."

Caleb met Thomas's gaze. He'd see the kid received a reward for his work. And he'd keep an eye on him with the future in mind. Reliable cowboys who not only stuck around but intuitively knew how to protect what the ranch owner valued were themselves invaluable. If Anchorman continued to mature along those lines, Caleb wanted to keep him around for the long haul.

For now, however, he left the kid in Thomas's capable hands and aimed for the main house, where he'd find Sallie. Anticipation and concern quickened his pace.

Doran had been here. He must have left Sallie upset, so much so that Mrs. Thomas allowed her into the main house, even the library. Mr. and Mrs. Thomas were the only people he ever allowed inside his domain. His sanctuary. Mrs. Thomas wouldn't have made an exception unless the situation called for it, even after he'd made the mistaken exception yesterday.

He launched up the back steps and plowed through the door to the kitchen.

"Mercy, Mr. Orson!" Mrs. Thomas dropped a large knife on the table. "Barging in here. What's wrong?"

"Where's Sallie?" he demanded, not caring how irritable he sounded.

Mrs. Thomas scowled and took the knife to the potatoes more forcefully than necessary. Did she imagine him as the potato? He cringed and apologized.

Mrs. Thomas huffed. "I gave her leave to look at your library. And don't you get angry with me neither. She was upset, her ankle paining her, and when she asked me for a book, I let her in to choose one. Girl hasn't emerged yet. Seems she likes that room as much as you do."

Caleb didn't know what to make of that, especially after their near kiss yesterday, which stalled the emotion boiling in his chest. Until his mind registered Sallie had been in pain.

He opened his mouth, however Mrs. Thomas wasn't finished. She wagged the knife at him. "And if you go barreling in there like a bull, I'll bar your way, I will. Leave the girl alone. She had to deal with Mr. Doran today. She doesn't need your ill-temper, too."

He let his jaw flop open, just like it had yesterday when Thomas had laid into him like a father would. The warmth of Mrs. Thomas's maternal actions caused words to form, but not ones he ever said. "You're right."

Her surprise raised her eyebrows nearly to her graying hairline. "What's this? Are you trying to play an April's Fool prank on me?"

Caleb snorted.

Mrs. Thomas cocked her head. "Then I do believe Sallie is wearing off on you. Kindness, dear boy, it does the heart good."

Kindness. Beauty. Love. He shuffled his feet, looking from door to door. One would lead him to the hall, and thus to the library, the other back outside and away from ... this. Her. No.

However, an impulse so unlike him had him speaking before he could change his mind. "Might I have a cutting of that purple flower just beginning to bloom in your garden?"

"The verbena?" Mrs. Thomas glanced toward where Sallie would be in the library, then back at him. "I think that is a marvelous idea."

Caleb smoothed his hair and beard as he waited for Mrs. Thomas to return with a handful of the purple flowers, his heart pounding. She smiled at him as he took them, a proud smile like that of a mother whose son did something right. He sure hoped he was doing so.

The flowers smelled fresh and light, and made him think of Sallie. "Thank you, Mrs. Thomas."

She emitted a happy sigh. "Who knew April Fools would turn you into a romantic? I approve."

"Mrs. Thomas." He growled, not liking the heat that prickled the back of his neck.

She laughed. "Go on with you now."

Caleb walked toward the library doors, each step seemingly heavier than the last. Was he doing the right thing? He switched the flower stems from one hand to the other to wipe a free one on a trouser leg. Yesterday, Sallie had followed him to ensure he was okay, even to the point of injuring herself—though before they left this morning, Thomas assured him the ankle wasn't strained. Still, the least he could do was return the favor. Make sure she was okay after having to interact with Doran, that her ankle had improved.

Maybe the flowers were too much and spoke of a future he couldn't promise.

Lord? The attempt at a prayer stalled in his chest. What was he doing? Bringing a girl flowers was not how a man stayed alone. And alone was for the best. He had too many scars. Too many broken pieces. War had left him too bereft to have anything left to give to a girl with a soul as beautiful as Sallie's.

He turned from the door. This idea was nothing but a horrible April Fool's prank and he wouldn't play one on Sallie. Or himself. *Perfect love ...* God's love ... Thomas's words from yesterday stalled him. During his momentary pause, he heard the doors open and froze.

"Caleb?" Sallie's voice.

He looked over his shoulder to where she stood framed in the library doorway. She wore her usual buckskin trousers with a blue shirt that reminded him of the Montana Territory sky. Soft brown hair was tied up in a ball at the back of her head, revealing a long, slender neck. Warm brown eyes met his own, pulling him and his heart toward her with their sense of peace and safety.

But he wasn't safe for her. He was a beast, so opposite her beauty. So, what did he do now?

Chapter Nine

Sallie held the book—*Voyage au centre de la terre* by Jules Verne—to her stomach and leaned against the door jamb to keep weight off her foot, though the rest had removed the pain, as she waited for Caleb's next move. If she wasn't mistaken, he'd meant to find her in the library but changed his mind. Now that he knew that *she* knew ... What would he decide?

"Did you find a book you liked?" Caleb turned slowly, keeping his hands behind his back and plenty of distance between them. His coat revealed the dirt of travel, his hair the ring left from his cowboy hat. His feet shuffled with nerves that reminded her of Arion.

She traced the edge of the book cover with her thumb, her forefinger trapped in the page she'd been reading. "*Voyage to the Center of the Earth.* The French is challenging to translate, and I can't speak it, but I've been teaching myself with a dictionary for the past several years so I can read authors like Alexandre Dumas and Victor Hugo."

Why was she talking so much? She couldn't be nervous, could she? No, no, this was about setting Caleb at ease and had nothing to do with him almost kissing her yesterday.

Caleb took a step nearer, his size dwarfing her. "You're teaching yourself a language?"

She shrugged, unable to meet his gaze. "Winter gets long in the cabin with only Papa for company." She smoothed her free hand down the worn leather of her trousers, wishing she'd packed a dress for once.

"Books make good companions. They don't make demands or expect conversation." He looked over her shoulder at the shelves lining his library. "It's why I've collected so many."

What should she say now? *Picture Arion.* She never had trouble thinking of something to say to one of her horses. But all she could think of was how it felt for him to carry her through the snow, for him to lean over and almost—

"I brought you something." He shifted from one foot to the other, then held out a fist full of delicate purple flowers. The citrus smell teased her nose.

"For me?" No one had ever brought her flowers before. As she took them from his large, rough hands, that little place of hurt deep in her heart flooded with a whole different feeling. Warm, like freshly baked bread. She ducked her head to blink away the sting of tears.

"Do you not like them?" Caleb touched her shoulder. Warm, comforting, safe.

"I like them very much." She pressed the flowers to her nose. Silence stretched between them, and Sallie couldn't think how to break it.

Caleb cleared his throat. "I'm sorry I wasn't here. When Doran found you."

That brought her attention to his face. The concern she saw there matched his tone, causing the ground to shift beneath her feet. She was used to being in command of a situation like this, not the recipient. She didn't know how to respond and stood frozen like a deer in a hunter's sight.

"You're uncomfortable." Caleb scratched his temple. "I'm not good at this, and after yesterday ... uh, maybe ... would you allow me to sit with you in the library? Mrs. Thomas is in the kitchen, so we won't be alone. And shouldn't you get off your ankle?"

Sallie lifted the flowers to her nose again, then nodded, she'd ask Mrs. Thomas for a vase later. For now, she wanted to be around him, even if everything felt awkward. Perhaps being surrounded by books would help loosen her tongue?

Caleb placed gentle fingers in the middle of her back, escorting her to the lone sofa. Behind it, the picture window showed the mountains to the west. The sun shone in, warming her shoulders as she sat.

"Did Doran harm you?" Caleb glanced at her leg as he perched on the edge of the sofa beside her as if ready to spring up at a moment's notice.

"No. I handled Mr. Doran." Not the whole truth. Sallie plucked a leaf and used it as a bookmark, setting both book and bouquet aside. *Focus on the horses.* "I was irritated because he undid all my work with Arion. The stable damage did enough of that, and I had Arion close to trusting me again. Then Mr. Doran barged in. Anyway, Mrs. Thomas invited me to choose a book from your library. I do hope that was all right."

"You're welcome to any book in here." He rubbed his thighs. "Perhaps you might also join me for supper tonight?"

Sallie's heart tripped. "I'll try not to chatter too much." He'd said he liked books because they didn't demand conversation.

His chin jerked up. "I like your chatter."

Salle touched her warm cheeks. Is this what having a beau felt like? It simultaneously made her giddy and terrified at the same time.

He scratched at his beard. "If you'd rather not ..."

"No." She didn't want him to rescind the invitation. "I mean, yes. I mean, I'd be delighted to join you for supper. Thank you."

The weathered skin of his cheeks bunched as he smiled. It took ten years off his face. What would it take to make that smile reach fully to his green eyes?

"I shall leave you to your book, Miss Beauregard." Caleb rose and bowed. "Until supper?"

Sallie looked up, taking in the large man with his broad shoulders, brown hair and beard, his worn shirt, and faded buckskin trousers. She marveled at how one man could give off a feeling of strength and safety while another made her feel small and uncomfortable. In

Caleb, she could see his pain, wanted to relieve it, and coaxed him to trust her.

"Sallie?" Question flickered across his features.

"Can you tell me more about Arion?" Sallie gave a self-deprecating chuckle. "Pardon my thought process. I'm simply curious."

"Uh, sure." Caleb returned to his seat on the sofa, and Sallie felt it a minor victory. "He was a wild horse once. I found him injured about eight months ago and brought him here. He wouldn't have survived the winter with his wounds and without his herd."

"What hurt him?" *Please, may it have been an animal, not a human.* Her father might be a trapper, but he never, never let an animal suffer.

Caleb rested his elbows on his knees. "Based on the bullet I had to take out of his shoulder? He had scrapes on his legs, too, like he ran into fencing in an attempt to escape. Didn't think I could save him, but I had to try."

She wanted to touch his shoulder, maybe hold his hand, but kept her fingers tangled in her lap. Yesterday, a touch seemed natural. Today, a touch seemed forward. "You're a good man, Caleb Orson."

"I'm not." He frowned. "What I had to do in war ... there's nothing *good* about it."

Now, she did reach for him, gripping his forearm, the heat of his skin reaching her palm through his heavy cotton sleeve. "What you had to do to survive in war has nothing to do with who you are as a person. Think of Arion. He might kick and bite and run in his fear and instinct to protect himself, but that doesn't make him a bad horse."

"It makes him broken. Dangerous."

Sallie tightened her hold on him as she shook her head, knowing full well they were talking about Caleb as much as Arion. "No one is beyond hope. Not Arion. Not Gunpowder. Not you."

His gaze trailed up her arm until it reached her eyes. "You really believe that."

Oh, how she disliked the bewilderment in his voice. "Of course I do, Caleb. I can see your heart. You took in an injured horse to heal him. You stand up to bullies like Mr. Doran. You unquestionably welcomed a talkative, socially awkward woman into your home as a favor to a mutual friend of her father. You. Are. A. Good. Man."

It came out of nowhere, his kiss. His scratchy whiskers on her chin, the gentle press of his lips on hers, the scent of evergreen swirling with his nearness—and just as quickly as it came, he was gone. From the sofa, from the room, from the house, if the slam of a distant door was any indication.

Sallie touched her fingers to her mouth. Her first kiss. And then she smiled.

· ❤ · ❤ · ❤ · ❤ · ❤ ·

He'd kissed her! Caleb stomped toward the corral where Duke grazed. How foolish could he be? He'd stopped himself yesterday.

But today? After Doran? After her expression of complete confidence in him?

Waving off a cowboy's offer of help, Caleb checked Duke's legs and hooves, then saddled and bridled the horse himself. He needed the connection to his old pal, the horse who had seen him through the war. Riding together would clear his head, wash away the confusion, and remind him of the soldier too battle-scarred for a mountain beauty like Sallie.

She thought he was good. Did a good man kiss a girl like that? Without permission, without intention to marry? She was innocent like the snow Duke's hooves cut through as they plotted a careful course toward the mountains.

What did a man like Caleb know of such things as innocence? He'd been raised in a modestly affluent home, sure. He knew society's expectations, though he could admit to stealing a kiss or two in his youth. But going to war meant losing that part of himself, losing the very definition of innocence. Taking a life, even in war, did that to a man.

April Fool indeed.

What Caleb wouldn't give for a long talk with Ahanu for the wisdom the older man imparted. Like Sallie, he'd seen a good man beneath the pain and welcomed Caleb into his family like a son. He gave him ownership of this land so it would remain in trusted hands when his people were undermined and sent to a reservation. Caleb felt that responsibility keenly. He was merely a caretaker, and he'd gladly give up his spread if Ahanu were here again.

The range's shadows stretched toward him like fingers. Reaching, grasping, haunting. Sallie was sunshine, casting away the darkness. But it was too deep. Too all-consuming. He'd simply snuff out her goodness. His soul was too empty. And yet, he craved her presence like a starving man does food.

Do you believe God loves you? Thomas's question echoed in his mind as Duke slowed to a halt. Caleb lifted his gaze to the place where the peaks touched the sky. "God?"

He dropped his chin. What could he ask? That Sallie would ... what? Become his wife? How could he ask that of her? To be bound to a man like him for the rest of her life? It was selfish. He had nothing to offer her. He'd only be taking, not giving, and despite his crusty soul, he knew that was no marriage.

And why was he thinking about marriage? Because of a kiss? Because of Thomas's words? Sallie didn't love him. He didn't love Sallie. The kiss was impulsive. Foolish. Sprung from attraction and a well of gratitude that responded to her goodness.

He patted Duke's neck, then crossed his wrists on the saddle horn. And yet, he couldn't help but see that Sallie was springtime to the winter in his soul. The promise of new life. And living in Montana these past years, he knew how long a winter could be. How wonderful spring felt ... It was a battle for warmth to push back winter's grip.

"Never good when I wax poetical, Duke." Caleb grunted and turned Duke toward home.

Yet the metaphor dogged his heels until he would have urged Duke into a gallop. If only they could see the ground under the snowpack. The recent thaw-freeze had ice hidden under the snow.

Dark and light. Winter and spring.

He glanced over his shoulder at the mountains. The sun glowed behind them, casting the plain in shadow but the peaks in brilliant glory. Draped in light, the snowcaps sparkled against the red-orange clouds. Caleb halted Duke. A gust swept across the rocks, swirling snow like a mist. Wild, beautiful, majestic.

I will lift up mine eyes unto the hills.

The words seemed to sweep down the mountain to wrap around him. Where were they from? He mentally scanned his library, searching the tomes he'd collected over the years. His stomach clenched. They were from the Bible. A book he hadn't cracked open since the war. But Sallie quoted it freely. As did the Thomases. Was this verse one she'd said while training Arion? She'd know the rest of it.

And suddenly, he wanted to know it, too. He urged Duke to return home as quickly as safety allowed. He handed the reins to one of his cowhands and hurried into the house. He'd asked Sallie to supper. He could ask her about the verse then. See if she was the one who had said it, planted it, as it were, in his head.

But the library was empty when he arrived. He made his way to the dining room. One place setting. Had he forgotten to tell Mrs. Thomas he'd invited Sallie to join him?

He entered the kitchen, the question on his tongue.

"You're late for supper." Mrs. Thomas didn't turn from the stove. "She went back to our house. She's not waiting on you and your moods. Now, do you want to eat?"

The hope that had momentarily spurred him home melted like spring snow. How had he so fully lost track of the time? Now he'd made a mess of it, as everyone should have expected. "I'm sorry, Mrs. Thomas. I know you worked hard, but I'm not hungry tonight."

She looked over her shoulder at him, eyes narrow, mouth pursed, but said nothing.

"I'm going out to check on the animals." Like he did whenever the restlessness came upon him.

There would be no sleep for him tonight.

Chapter Ten

Sallie blinked as she stared up at the ceiling beams from her bed in the Thomases' guest room, the world still dark. What had woken her?

She propped up on her elbows. No rain or ice or snow hit the window glass. In fact, a moonbeam perfectly shown through, like a beacon aimed at the flowers on the bureau. She smiled at them, remembering Caleb's nervousness. His kiss. She knew it hadn't meant more than mere gratefulness, but it was an action she'd carry with her. Treasure. Perhaps she'd dry the flowers and keep them in her Bible to remember to pray for Caleb when she left the ranch.

Left the ranch.

She sighed and plopped back. She missed her father and her cabin in the mountains, but she didn't miss living in a tent for months and months. Then there was Caleb's library. She could get used to visiting that room every day, lined with so many books as it was—ordering all of them from out East must have taken a fortune—not only that, she felt safe and cozy in that room.

She rubbed her eyes, rolled over, and burrowed under the quilt. Was it the books or the feeling that Caleb often spent time in his library that gave it that warm feeling? She sighed. Oh, Caleb. The poor man had scared himself with that kiss, which made it, and him, even more endearing. She hadn't stayed around for supper, though he'd invited her. No need to pressure him into keeping an awkward arrangement. Mrs. Thomas would have told him where to find her if he had desired her company. But Sallie had watched the stable and knew he hadn't returned until after supper. As skittish as a wild horse.

A noise came from the main room. Though it was the middle of the night, Mr. or Mrs. Thomas must be moving about. That must have been what woke her. She closed her eyes, but her heart ached. The day would come, but she didn't want to leave this place. Silly thought. Of course, she would leave when her father returned.

A shout had her sitting up. She swung her feet out of bed and grabbed the wrap Mrs. Thomas had loaned her as the cold caused a shiver to run down her spine. She went to the window. Her breath fogged the glass, and she wiped it away. Fear skittered down her spine at the sight of torches headed their way. She shed her nightgown in a flash and donned her buckskin trousers, coat, and boots. Tugging her knit cap over her braided hair, she left her room.

"You stay right here, Sallie Beauregard." Mrs. Thomas pointed a finger at her. The older woman hugged a wrap around her nightgown, her gray hair loose around her shoulder. "It's not safe outside tonight."

Obviously. But she kept that thought to herself.

"What's going on?" Sallie went to the window. If the horses were in danger, she'd disregard Mrs. Thomas's instructions in a heartbeat.

"I don't know. Mr. Thomas has gone out to see." Mrs. Thomas paced, her slippers slapping the wood floor. "Men with torches. Many men."

"It'll be alright." Sallie intercepted her host, hands to her shoulders, attempting to portray an assurance she didn't feel. "It's never smart to rush into danger. Once we know what's going on, we can respond."

Mrs. Thomas raised an eyebrow. "I should be telling you that, young lady."

Sallie shrugged, hoping it hid her worry. "Living in the wild, it's a lesson I learned early on at my father's knee. Running about simply makes us prey."

"Is that *pray* with an *A* or *prey* with an *E*?" Mrs. Thomas tugged her to the table. "Nevermind. *Pray* with an *A* is a good idea."

Sallie obliged because she could tell the older woman needed the quiet moment, but Sallie wasn't one for traditional prayer. The nomadic life hadn't brought her into church very often. Instead, nature served as her cathedral. Papa, her pastor. The animals, her fellow congregants. And God, her Friend. One didn't require folded hands or bent knees to carry on a conversation. Perhaps that made Sallie a heathen, as other women had scolded, telling her father his child would go wayward when they missed church weeks at a time. Not that Papa had let their criticism change their ways.

With half an ear to the growing commotion outside, she gripped Mrs. Thomas's hands and attempted to follow along to the woman's prayer. However, her own thoughts trampled the older woman's words. Concern for the animals, for Gunpowder and Arion, and Caleb, too. Why were men converging on the ranch at this time of night and in so militant a fashion?

As soon as Mrs. Thomas uttered an *amen*, Sallie was on her feet. She couldn't wait any longer. "I'll be back, Mrs. Thomas." Before her hostess could stop her, Sallie was out the door.

She halted on the porch, stunned. Had half of Blue Spruce brought torches to Crooked Tooth? Why?

"Doran!" a shout from the crowd cut through the noise. Of course, Doran was behind this. Cocky man. "There she is!"

Wait, her? She bounced on her toes, ready for flight. *Don't be prey.*

"Leave her alone!" Caleb bounded around the crowd, putting himself between the men and her. She didn't relax, but she breathed easier. Caleb exuded strength and protection. A bear ready to defend her. She'd explore why that tugged at her stomach later.

"You kidnapped her!" A man in a rumpled suit jabbed his finger at Caleb. The mayor of Blue Spruce was here?

"Kidnapped?" The word slipped from her lips. This made no sense whatsoever!

Caleb backed toward her, reaching behind to take her hand in his. Calloused and rough but strong, and that strength went straight to her heart. "I did not kidnap Sallie Beauregard. She's here of her own free will."

"And you call me a ruiner of reputations!" Doran laughed, slapping the mayor's shoulder. Oh, she did not like that man! "Made her your mistress, have you? Or do you plan to make an honest woman out of her?"

Of all the mortifying—

"Do not besmirch her good name!" Caleb roared, lurching forward. Sallie tightened her grip to keep him from launching himself at Doran. Fisticuffs would not help this situation. Though his defense of her nearly put stars in her eyes. She bit her lip. She wasn't a moon-eyed girl, but Caleb's actions threatened to sweep her off her feet.

Stand firm, Sal. The last thing she needed was for any of these men to see her softness toward Caleb. Doran, especially, would see that as a weakness to exploit.

"The missus and I are her chaperones." Mr. Thomas pushed through the crowd to stand between the men and Caleb. "This is my house. My wife and I are seeing to her, per her father's request. You do not need to fear for Miss Beauregard. She is in safe hands."

She was safe. But as lovely as they were, Mr. and Mrs. Thomas weren't why she felt that way. Not that she'd say so. She resisted leaning closer to Caleb. That would only make things worse.

"How do we know that for sure?" Doran sneered and wagged his finger at Caleb. "Rumor is she was in that man's house today."

Oh mercy. Sallie's cheeks heated at the insinuation, but she refused to duck her head. She'd done nothing wrong! However unease slithered up her spine. Who had been watching her? Was one of the cowhands a traitor to Caleb, snitching to Doran, of all people? Betrayal stung.

"She was with me in the house." Mrs. Thomas appeared beside Sallie. She tugged her away from Caleb, wrapping an arm protectively around her shoulder. Sure, it was a wise move, but it left Sallie feeling cold. "I'm Mr. Orson's cook and Sallie's guardian. I thank you to stop spreading rumors that will cost this girl her character. Nothing untoward is happening here. Is that understood?"

Several of the men shuffled under Mrs. Thomas's schoolmarm tone. One, however, squared off.

"And Miss Beauregard is never alone?" Doran hissed like a serpent. "Never unattended, unchaperoned? A stranger couldn't have a private moment with her?"

Sallie shuddered. Is that the real reason Doran visited the ranch earlier today? Or was this retribution for Sallie turning down his marriage proposal again? Or perhaps both reasons were true. Ugh. This is why she spent her time with animals. They didn't make her feel small and shamed. She never felt she needed to hide herself like she did right now. Her eyes prickled.

However, Caleb relaxed, and then he ... grinned? "Ah, Doran, that is where you're wrong."

His deep voice rumbled. Was that a laugh? It settled in Sallie's chest, loosening the tension.

Caleb crossed his arms and leaned a hip against the porch post. "I know you made an unsanctioned and unwelcome visit to my ranch today, Doran. Do you think you were left unsupervised? Especially when you spoke to Miss Beauregard in the corral? Scaring my horses as she was training them."

Murmurs rose through the crowd and Sallie straightened. Caleb had someone looking out for her? It was the only way *he* knew the details of what went on.

Caleb ran his gaze over the crowd and settled on the mayor. "I see Doran didn't mention that, did he? Gentleman, I'm surprised at you. Don't you recall it's April Fools? What's that saying, Miss Beauregard? Pulling the wool ..." He turned to her, beckoning, bringing her into the conversation.

She caught onto his plan. If the men thought this was all a big joke, maybe they wouldn't listen to Doran so easily next time. She stepped beside him. "Do you mean 'pull the wool over your eyes' or to 'hoodwink' someone? Both could be a form of an April Fool's prank."

"Yes, thank you." Caleb smiled at her, causing a balloon to fill her chest. Then he faced the crowd. Confidence and steel in his bearing. It'd be intimidating if Sallie didn't know there was a soft spot deep in his heart where he never let any light shine. "So you see, gentleman, Doran pulled one over on you, and me. However, I do not approve of risking a young woman's reputation for sport. See that it doesn't happen again."

"I'm terribly sorry, Miss Beauregard." The mayor stepped forward, hat covering his chest. "You have our sincerest apologies. We thought you were here under duress and came to save you. It's the least we could do for your father. He's been a loyal part of our community for longer than I've been here."

Sallie attempted her most sincere smile. She needed these men to trust her and Caleb, not Doran. "Thank you for your concern, sir. You can be assured this is where my father sent me. I'm perfectly safe and happy."

Caleb stepped from the porch, leading his men to herd the crowd toward the road back to town. Doran, however, stayed put, his expression growing darker the further away the townsmen went. He and Caleb stared each other down for a full minute like two stallions preparing to battle. Sallie bristled. She wasn't a breed mare for those two to fight over. She neither needed them to flash their pretty feathers nor fight to the death. If she wanted a husband, the choice would be hers.

Doran glanced at her, smirked, and then allowed a cowhand to direct him toward town. Sallie clenched her teeth. Dastardly man. He had wanted a reaction from her and she'd given it to him.

Mrs. Thomas tugged Sallie toward the house, but Sallie still caught Caleb's low words to Mr. Thomas. "Find the traitor and dismiss him."

"Understood, boss." Mr. Thomas nodded. "Loyal cowhands only."

Inside, Mrs. Thomas fussed over Sallie, getting her tea and a snack before she settled under the quilt. Sallie allowed the older woman to take care of her because it seemed Mrs. Thomas needed it to calm her own nerves. But once the house went quiet, Sallie returned to the window.

A cloud blocked the moonbeams but not the light. She watched Caleb stalk from the cow barn to the pasture fence to the paddock. Could she feel his restlessness from here? Or was that her imagination? She wanted to go to him and tell him things would be okay. A lie, surely. One situation had been diffused, but she feared Doran would only escalate from here. He'd provoke Caleb, unleash the beast in order to destroy him. And Sallie had handed Doran the means.

Sallie stepped away from the window and sat on the edge of the bed. Her gaze snagged on the flowers Caleb had given her earlier that day. She rose to trace the petals with a finger. She cared for Caleb, though she didn't know what that meant. His defense of her, his nervousness when asking her to a supper he'd scared himself from attending ... She suspected he cared for her as well.

If not for Doran, perhaps they could explore what that meant. She felt connected to Caleb, as she had to Gunpowder from that first day. Could she get Caleb to trust her as she did with her horses? She leaned into the flowers, letting the scent fill her senses. She wanted to hold on to that connection more than she dreamed.

And that's why she needed to leave.

If she didn't remove herself from Doran's sight, Caleb or his men could be injured—or worse—defending her. She would never let that happen.

Chapter Eleven

Caleb stood in the shadow of a large ponderosa, watching Sallie work with Arion. She'd taken the stallion to a back pasture, away from the noise of rebuilding the stable. It'd been two days since Doran had led that mob onto his property, yet Caleb hadn't worked up the courage to talk to her about it or apologize for missing their dinner together.

Truth was, he didn't know what to do, a rare occurrence for him. Having her here risked her reputation, but sending her away tore at something inside. And either way, she wasn't safe.

"You asked for me, sir?" Anchorman approached, keeping to fallen pine leave to quiet his steps. He nodded to where Sallie worked with Arrion. "Keeping out of her attention?"

Smart kid. "She doesn't need to know about this." Neither he nor Thomas had unearthed the traitor who shared information with Doran. The cowhands were all strangely mum.

Anchorman crossed his arms. "What do you need me to do?"

Caleb kept his gaze on Sallie. She was at the point of introducing Arion to a saddle blanket. "If you wanted information, would you bribe a cowhand or send in a spy?"

"I don't think it's that simple, sir." The kid pulled his cowboy hat low over his eyes. "Thomas's questions have everyone on alert, but Doran is ... wily. He uses the girls in his employ."

Caleb studied him out of the corner of his eye. "And how do you know this?"

"Because one approached me last night." The kid cleared his throat. "I went to town to see if I could find answers for you. I did, and I don't think it's as simple as a single cowboy. The women are collecting little pieces of truth. Doran puts that information together, sprinkles in some fear and exaggeration, and then poisons the men in his saloon with it."

Caleb massaged his neck. "What would the men say if I restricted them to the ranch?"

"It's not the men you'd have to worry about. Doran would paint you a warden." Anchorman scratched his brow. "I think you're best off keeping Miss Beauregard's movements as hidden as possible."

Caleb snorted. "She won't abide that." Unless he locked her in the library, but then someone would whisper about that. He rubbed his eyes. This was an impossible situation. Anything he did would affect her.

"Sir? Have you considered marrying her?"

"What?" Caleb growled—impertinent kid. Yet the idea sparked something cheerful in Caleb's chest. It made him even grouchier.

"Sorry, sir, it's just that if she were married, Doran couldn't marry her. You could keep her safe in the main house without risking her reputation." He shrugged. "I know I ain't got no experience in that area, being a fresh-faced youth and all, but I seen the way you look at her. Like my pa looked at my ma before they passed."

"Carl." The warning in Caleb's tone only brought out the kid's grin.

"I also think she knows we're here." Anchorman nodded toward where Sallie glanced over her shoulder so quickly that Caleb would have missed it had he not been watching. "I'll keep my ears open and report in. I like Miss Beauregard, sir. She's good to us cowhands. Not that it's my business, but I'm grateful to you for this job and respect you. She makes you happy."

"Noted, kid." Caleb didn't know what to do with any of that. "Report to me or Thomas if you learn anything."

"Aye, aye." Anchorman gave a two-finger salute and disappeared. Caleb stepped away from the tree and approached Sallie.

"I wondered how long you'd stand there before saying hello. And that conversation with Mr. Anchorman looked intense." Sallie rubbed Arion's neck, one hand on the horse's halter. She didn't look at Caleb as she spoke. "Isn't that right, Arion? Uh-hum. I agree. Not to mention, your owner has been sullen since Saturday night. But not you, handsome boy. You let me brush you and put your saddle blanket on. Such a good boy. Shall we see if you'll let your owner near?"

Caleb shook his head. Anchorman thought he should marry her. What could a sullen man like Caleb offer someone like her? "Nice work with him." The compliment sounded too stern to be an encouragement.

She raised her eyebrow as she glanced over her shoulder at him. His breath stalled. How could a woman be so beautiful in worn buckskin trousers and dust-encrusted shirt? He folded his arms.

Sallie laughed. "Come on, Arion ol' boy. We'll show your owner how it's done."

Against his better judgment, he stayed still. Sallie walked beside Arion, leading him toward Caleb. Arion nodded his head and nudged Sallie's arm. Sallie responded with a pat. In moments, they reached Caleb. He was a horseman, a cavalryman, but he had no idea what to do next.

Sallie led Arion so his flank faced Caleb, then she gently took his large, calloused hand and lifted it to Arion's neck. Her touch froze Caleb. Arion's skin rippled. His tail flicked. His ears turned toward Sallie's soft words. Were those murmurs for Arion or Caleb? "That's it. Slowly. You two will be pals again in no time." Sallie moved Caleb's hand along Arion's neck.

"Sallie." Caleb's words caught in his throat as she placed the lead rope in his hands. The woman muddled every coherent thought in his head.

She stepped away. "I think Arion is settled now. You should be able to take over his training and get a saddle on him if you so desire. Stallions are notorious for causing trouble, but I think he'll be a good stud horse. And manageable now, if you keep working with him."

Wait, what was she saying? Why did it sound like instructions a person gave before they left?

"He's not ready to ride yet, but he has the potential to get there. And since his purpose isn't for riding, you can exercise him in a corral until then." She was backing away from both of them.

Arion stepped after her. Caleb followed. "You can keep working with Arion. I'm not here to stop you." Is that what she thought? Is that what his sullenness had caused?

She wouldn't meet his gaze. A skittish animal if he ever saw one. But why? Had Doran gotten into her head? Was standing her up for dinner after he kissed her that significant? Probably. And didn't that hurt? He ruined any chance he had before he decided he wanted one. Wait, did he want one? Or was that Thomas or Anchorman in his head?

"Sallie, do you miss your father?" Was that it?

"Of course I do." Her smile was soft. "And I'll miss being here."

"You can't leave." He swallowed back the panic, not wanting to upset Arion. "It's not safe. Doran—I won't let anything happen to you."

"I know, Caleb. I know. I have felt completely safe and welcome here. And you have been a perfect gentleman." She met his gaze then, her meaning clear. She saw that goodness in him. Didn't think him a cad or scoundrel. Then why was she pulling away from him? Her breath hitched. "Don't you see, that is why I have to leave. I am grateful for everything you've done for me. Please. I ... I will never forget you."

Caleb squinted at her as if that could help him read behind her words. She was shoving him away. She planned to leave the ranch, but not because she felt unsafe. Not because of him. Though, there was one way to test that last assumption. He darted out an arm, wrapped it around her waist, and tugged her to him. She squealed and planted her hand against his chest.

"Caleb!" She gasped and did not pull away. Yup, she wasn't running because of him. It warmed his heart and gave him the courage to fight for her, for them.

"I had a theory to test, Miss Beauregard. And perhaps one more."

"Caleb." she chewed her lip. "I need to leave. Doran won't stop, and I can't bear to see—"

He kissed her, and she melted in his arms. For a glorious moment, the world ceased to exist. Then Arion nosed them.

"Oh, you silly horse." Sallie gave a breathless laugh.

"That won't get you any oats from me," Caleb grumbled. He cupped Sallie's cheek, realizing he'd dropped Arion's lead during that kiss. "Sallie, I don't want you to leave. I can handle Doran. But you. I'm terrified I'm going to hurt you. I'm a broken man. You are sunshine and spring flowers. What do I have to offer you?

"You have more to offer than you think. But that's not why I'm leaving. And I am leaving, Caleb." She pulled away then. "That kiss told me just how important it is for me to do so."

He followed her. "What do you mean? How could that kiss say that?"

"Because I care about you too much to let Doran hurt you." Tears turned her brown eyes into deep, glistening ponds. "He will hurt you, Caleb. He knows I'm your weakness, and you are mine. We cannot let him win. If I'm not here, he'll lose interest in me. I'm no longer something to fight with you over."

Her reasoning made too much sense. "I'm a selfish man, Sallie, I don't want to lose you." Frankly, he wasn't sure he would survive her absence. Just the thought of it was like dousing the sun.

She returned to him, a compassionate smile clearing her tears. "Do not put yourself down, Caleb Orson. You are not the beast you think you are. God made you. He knows every broken part of you. Let Him shine light in those dark places. Then you won't need me."

Her words stabbed, ripped, and opened his heart to a blinding flash he hadn't expected. Then she tugged his shirt so his lips met hers and only her kiss kept his knees from buckling.

"This isn't goodbye, Caleb." She handed him Arion's lead rope, but her chin quivered. "It can't be, which is why I'm leaving before you get hurt."

"Sallie."

But she was too quick for him this time. She darted away, and Caleb leaned his head against Arion's neck, his heart breaking in half.

·♥·♥·♥·♥·♥·

Sallie left a note for Caleb in his library, then wrapped the morning's biscuits in a napkin and placed them in her saddlebag. The day was nearing its end, but she'd lose her nerve if she didn't leave now. That kiss had nearly been her undoing. She just couldn't let any harm come to Caleb. She couldn't.

Her heart breaking, she turned Gunpowder toward the mountains. She didn't have a plan beyond gathering supplies back at her family's mountain cabin. Somehow, she had to stay out of sight until Doran lost interest. Or could she actively find a way to get him to back off? Even then, Doran hated Caleb. He'd find another reason to provoke him. She needed to end their battle for good. But how?

A deep sigh worked its way up from the aching place in her soul. If anyone was selfish, it was her. She didn't want to leave Caleb. She wanted to heal him, but that wasn't her place. That's why she left the note. Perhaps, by the time she figured this out, she and Caleb would be ready to explore the connection that seemed to tether them.

But weren't two heads better than one?

The thought worried at her soul as she rode, like an ill-fitting shoe. Her horses were the only creatures to which she could relate the concept. She and Gunpowder acted as one. Together, they were stronger. But how did that work with people? Papa never asked for her advice about trapping animals or when to strike camp. She followed because she knew nothing else, until he left her at Caleb's ranch.

When she worked with a horse, it also didn't involve another human. It was her and the horse, building a relationship and trust.

She scratched underneath her knit hat. Wasn't that what she'd done with Caleb? She'd always seen him as a wild horse. Had she managed to build trust with him? His kiss said maybe she had. But had she destroyed it by leaving?

The unsettled feeling churned her stomach. She brought Gunpowder to a halt and turned him so she could look back down the mountain. She was just over halfway to the cabin. Her spirit tugged her back toward Crooked Tooth, back toward Caleb. Was it better to fight Doran together? Should she turn around or continue on her course?

Her indecision froze her. The wind blew a top layer of snow into her face. She brushed it away and looked up the mountain. Panic squeezed her chest. She'd been so lost in thought she had failed to pay attention. Clouds had built up over the peaks. The kind that promised snow, and lots of it.

Another gust of wind, cold and biting, tried to cut through her buckskin coat. A spring snowstorm. It would sweep down the mountains, trapping her and Gunpowder before she made it to Papa's cabin. Could she beat the snow back down to the valley? Back to Crooked Tooth? Though the cabin was closer, she could face blinding snow either way.

Worse, she was on her own. No Papa. No Caleb. And her choice could mean life or death for both her and her horse.

Chapter Twelve

Caleb took a late midday meal in his library. Thomas could run the ranch without him and Anchorman should return soon from his daily ride into town. The kid had let the barkeep at Doran's saloon think him an irresponsible boy escaping work to stare at the ladies over luncheon. Other than reporting Doran's darkening moods, he hadn't uncovered the man's source yet.

They needed to act swiftly so Sallie could return. Caleb set the plate, littered with the rest of his uneaten cold meat and bread on a side table in order to pace. He'd always loved this room, but now it reminded him of Sallie. Her absence had stolen his appetite, but he felt her comfort here. Perhaps it would enlighten him to a way to end this feud with Doran.

He walked from one end of the room to the other, hands behind his back. Instead of strategy, his mind conjured images of her. Galloping beside Arion as she brought him to a halt in that buckskin outfit of hers. The peace she emanated as she calmed his terrified horse. The fire in her eyes that first night as she defended Arion and then the pain when she realized her father had left her here.

Under Caleb's protection.

Nothing about letting Sallie go said it was best for her protection. In fact, he fought against every instinct not to jump on Duke and race after her. His pacing increased. Her father trusted Caleb to look out for her. To keep her safe from Doran. No doubt about it. Caleb had failed.

Have you considered marrying her? Anchorman's question came back to him.

As if that's what her father wanted when he left her here.

His path around the library brought him to his desk, where *Voyage au centre de la terre* by Jules Verne still sat after Sallie had left it there ... with a paper sticking out of its pages? He opened the cover to find a folded paper with his name on it.

What was this?

My dear Caleb,

His gaze dropped to the signature. Sallie.

His heart gave an uneasy bump, and he leaned against a bookcase, angling the paper toward the window. It made her parting words push into his mind. *God made you. He knows every broken part of you. Let Him shine light in those dark places.* The thought echoed what he'd been considering the other day. He let the words settle against the cracked places deep inside, the wounds he'd hidden since the war. But Sallie had seen them.

My dear Caleb,

I couldn't return home without giving you a lamp to light your way. One of my favorite verses comes from Isaiah, chapter nine, verse two: "The people that walked in darkness have seen a great light: they that dwell in the land of the shadow of death, upon them hath the light shined." In chapter sixty, Isaiah says, "Arise, shine; for thy light is come, and the glory of the Lord is risen upon thee." Jesus is this light. He can bring you out of the darkness, dear Caleb. You can trust Him.

Prayerfully yours,

Sallie

Caleb ran his thumb over Sallie's handwriting, a beautiful script that fit a beautiful soul. How could he be worthy of joining her in the light?

He read over the verse again, his gaze stalling on the phrase, *they that dwell in the land of the shadow of death*. That was where he lived. It surrounded him. Haunted him. Chained him to the past. And yet, it was upon those that the light shined. Not the good, not those surrounded by life. No, those that dwelt in the shadow of death.

Stunned, he leaned back against the hard edges of the shelf to absorb the concept. It wasn't the worthy that the light shined on, but those surrounded by darkness and death—the broken. The people like him who despaired that morning would come. That winter would end.

He closed his eyes. Inhaled. Then let out his breath. Slow. Steady. Accepting. Trusting. And peace flooded him, the like of which he hadn't felt since before the war, perhaps not even then.

"Caleb!" Thomas's knock at the library door nearly muffled his shout. "Anchorman is back and he has news."

Caleb set aside the letter and threw open the library door. "Where is he?"

"Steps behind me." Thomas led them out to the porch where Anchman met them along with a cold wind.

It had been a beautiful morning, but how long had he been in the library? Spring weather could turn quickly. He glanced toward the mountains. Grey snow clouds hid the peaks in a heavy cloak. Caleb's throat convulsed. "Sallie."

Anchoman's eyes widened as he turned toward the west and gathering storm. "Boss ... Doran went after Miss Beauregard. Erman told him she was headed up the mountain alone."

Caleb's chest seized. She was going home. In a storm. With Doran on her heels.

"Erman?" Thomas huffed. The cowhand who had abused his horse. Of course he was the snitch. Didn't matter. Caleb had to reach Sallie before Doran. "That two-faced—"

He interrupted his foreman. "Do you know where Beauregard lives?"

"Other than up in the mountains?" Thomas waved at the storm about to sweep down into the valley.

Fear shot through Caleb. He slapped Anchorman's shoulder. "Get Duke ready, then sit and catch your breath. Thomas, have your wife pack supplies. I'm going after Sallie." Then he turned to run inside to dress for a snowstorm. And a fight.

"You can't face both Doran and the snow alone," Thomas hollered after him.

Caleb glanced back. "I won't demand my men follow me into danger."

"Who said you had to demand it?" Thomas' words followed Caleb up the stairs. "What if if they're willing?"

He nearly missed the top step. Willing? That level of loyalty could only be due to Sallie. He donned his warmest clothes, then strapped on a pair of knives and two pistols. Snow, Doran, or any other danger aside, he'd find Sallie, and then he'd convince her to stay on the ranch as his wife because he didn't want to face the future without her by his side.

Sallie hunkered into her coat as she let Gunpowder guide her down the mountain. They'd been making good progress on the old avalanche path until the snow started flying. Gusts of white whipped by, hiding the world behind an impenetrable curtain. In those moments, she halted Gunpowder, unwilling to risk injury or his life should he step wrong. But staying on the mountain wasn't an option either, not without shelter.

How had a trapper's daughter, who lived her whole life as a nomad in the mountains, not seen this coming? Though the answer was so simple, she couldn't help but scold herself. She'd been distracted. Instead of respecting nature and the mountains, she'd let her concern for Caleb and her fear of Doran dictate her choices. And now it could cost her horse his life. And hers.

"I'm sorry, Gunpowder. I know better."

But did she? Doubt crept in with another gust of snow. When had she ever navigated the mountains alone? And when it came to men, what experience did she have? She'd never had a beau. She never had a man interested in marrying her. Her father's protection had left her safe but naive. She followed him through the wilderness, but now that she was alone ...

This observation shook her. Never had she felt such a lack of confidence before. It mixed with fear and threatened to swirl into panic, which was deadly in the wild. She halted Gunpowder and examined her surroundings. Evergreens lined the wide path, their tall spires reaching into the gray above. The path was dotted with fallen limbs and debris from the avalanche that first created it.

She thought she could help Caleb find the light, but who was she to help him when she felt just as lost? No, not lost exactly. Alone. So alone. Always needing someone to keep her from getting lost, it seemed. To keep her safe.

Yet I am not alone because the Father is with me.

Jesus' words from the book of John rose from within her. She squeezed her eyes closed to see the passage. Slowly, the image filtered into her mind in bits and pieces.

The Father is with me ... ye might have peace ... be of good cheer ...

She was not alone because God was with her. She bowed her head. The snow fell on her shoulders. She wasn't alone. God would never leave her. And now it was time to get down the mountain. Return to Caleb. Put an end to Doran's harassment. Together this time.

She urged Gunpowder forward again. One step at a time, he inched toward the valley. But the storm moved faster, harder. It covered her and Gunpowder in wet snow. It whipped across her face, stinging her cheeks. The wind pushed at her from behind, threatening to unseat her. *Lord, I need help.*

Onward, they plodded. Careful steps that would wear Gunpowder down well before they reached the valley. She fought against the worry and prayed for the wind to lessen. That's when she heard the bells. Like those sometimes attached to a harness. And a male voice calling her name.

Caleb? Had Caleb come after her? *Thank you, Lord!*

Sallie halted Gunpowder and stood in the stirrups, waving her arms. "Here! I'm here!" She never wanted to kiss a man as much as she did this instant.

Out of the swirling snow, a large man emerged. But he didn't ride Duke, and Sallie's joy turned to dread. Doran. How had he found her in this snow? How had he even known she left the ranch? Did he mean to trap her in her cabin only for the snow to change his plans?

"I've come to save you," Doran shouted into the wind. "Follow me."

Nothing Doran did was for anyone other than himself. He'd tracked her for a reason. Yet, she'd never faced the mountain alone, especially not with a storm like this. Dare she trust him to lead her to relative safety? She didn't, but what choice did she have?

"I don't know why Orson let you out in a snowstorm." Doran came alongside her. Coated in a layer of sticky flakes, he looked like a snow beast. "He's not good enough for you."

"And you are?" The snapping words battled the doubt Doran's words whispered into her soul. "I'm sorry."

"I've told you my intentions from the beginning." Doran's gloved hand covered her forearm. "I aim to marry you. You need a keeper, Sal, and I'll take care of you. We'll go to town, get married, and tell your father when he returns."

"What?" Sallie stared at him for a moment, then yanked away, causing Gunpowder to shift sideways toward the evergreens and the tree-wells beneath them. Her heart rate picked up, stealing her breath. "I don't need a keeper!"

Yet maybe she did. Tears and icy snow stung her eyes. She'd gotten herself into this mess.

Doran didn't follow her, only shouted through the storm. "After we hole up together because of the snow, you'll have to marry me to save your reputation. It's already been questioned. You're getting a name for yourself, Sal. Only a man like me will accept you now."

That band of panic around her chest slid up to encompass her throat. He'd meant to trap her, and the snow only aided him. She should have stayed on the ranch. With Caleb. Why did she think she could protect him by leaving? Naive girl. All sunshine and roses. Now look at her.

Doran's laugh echoed around her. "I've chosen you to be my beautiful trophy, Sal Beauregard. And I will have you. Not even Orson will stop me, or I'll kill him."

No, no, no! "I won't marry you!" Sallie shouted at him. She turned Gunpowder away from Doran, away from the avalanche path, and toward the trees. They'd make a trail where there wasn't one and hope the snow could hide them until they could safely find the valley.

"I'll just follow you, Sal." Doran's words did just that.

"Not if I have anything to say about it." Caleb! She halted Gunpowder ten feet from the trees. Caleb appeared out of the snow astride Duke like the cavalryman he was, coming to save her from Doran. And she loved him for it.

"You can't have her." Doran angled his horse toward her.

Caleb did the same. Behind him, several men emerged from the fog of snow, Mr. Thomas and young Anchorman at the front. These men came looking for her. Surely Doran wouldn't try to keep her now, not with this show of strength.

In an instant, she could imagine the future. Life on the ranch beside Caleb, loyal cowboys like Thomas and Anchorman working the horses and cattle alongside them. Warm meals made by the loving hands of Mrs. Thomas. Quiet evenings in the library, just Sallie and Caleb. Teaching children to ride. Exploring the mountains. Raising the colts born from Arion. Papa visiting when he came through the area and teaching his grandchildren about the animals he tracked and how to preserve their meat and pelts.

Yes, it sounded like heaven nestled on a ranch called Crooked Tooth, and she wanted it wholeheartedly.

Except Doran pulled a pistol and aimed it at Caleb, just as Caleb's pistol cleared his holster.

"No!" she shouted.

Gunshots sounded. Sallie screamed. And then a violent crack rent the air, followed by an increasing roar.

Sallie's gaze shot up the mountain. She didn't need to see the cornice collapse to know what had just happened.

They'd set off an avalanche.

Chapter Thirteen

Pain speared Caleb's stomach. Doran's bullet had found its mark. A roar filled his ears. Blood? No. Avalanche.

Sallie! His men! "Run!" The word ripped from his throat as the pain nearly knocked him from Duke. He clutched the saddle horn.

The next instant, Sallie, on Gunpowder, reached his side. She grabbed Duke's bridle. "Come on. Come on. To the trees. We have to get out of the path."

The snow spiraled around him. Where were Thomas, Anchorman, and Doran? He tried to look but felt himself tilting off Duke. He tightened his hold and pressed his heels into the stirrups. Duke high-stepped beside Sallie and Gunpowder, and the motion shot a blinding white-hot pain through his torso.

Caleb clamped a hand beneath his ribs. Felt the blood. A gut shot? His chances of survival were low. "Sallie, go on. I'll catch you." Though he knew he wouldn't.

"Just stay on your horse," Sallie yelled back at him—stubborn woman. "You hear me, Caleb? Don't you give up."

The roar grew louder. Snow and sound whirled around him. Sallie and Gunpowder picked up speed. Duke followed suit. Caleb forced his eyes open despite the pain, despite the snow.

Trees cracked on the mountain above them as a whole shelf of snow slid toward them as if on skids. Closer, faster, it swept toward them. Sallie's encouragement grew louder, more urgent, until drowned by the roar of snow. Fifteen feet to safety. Ten. Five.

Caleb bent low over his saddle, nearly gripping Duke's neck to stay on his back. The pain, the blood loss, it cast him in darkness. No, no, not true darkness. Here in this valley of death, the light had come. If he died, he'd see Jesus. *Just please keep Sallie safe.* That's all he asked. And his men.

"Thomas?" He forced the question out. Sallie didn't answer. She couldn't hear him even if he'd even managed to speak his foreman's name aloud. *God, please let my men have gotten clear.*

Finally, trees loomed close even as snow billowed toward them, pouring, tumbling, consuming down the path it had taken once before. Gunpowder and Duke stepped into the shelter of the evergreens. *Thank you, God.* And then the darkness swept him off his horse.

·❤·❤·❤·❤·❤·

Sallie urged Gunpowder and Duke into one last surge, only for the movement to knock Caleb from the saddle. She snagged Caleb's lariat from Duke's saddle, let the horses go free—their instincts would keep them safe—and slung the rope around a tree. A moment later, the snow block rushed past them, spraying snow, dirt, and rock. Sallie tucked Caleb's head against her middle and held on to the rope to keep them from tumbling down with the snow.

The tree trunk blocked the worst of the avalanche's spray, but by the time it slowed, only Sallie's head was above the snow. Before the snow hardened, she made space around Caleb's face for him to breathe and freed her hands. Her heart pounded in her ears, all the louder for the silence that came after the slide. The pines sheltered them from the snowstorm, but it did little to bring peace to her spirit. Snow turned to ice around her chest even as she attempted to scrape it away from her body. Time was of the essence. She had to dig Caleb out. Find out why he'd fallen off his horse. That wasn't like Caleb, which meant something was wrong.

What about Caleb's men? Mr. Thomas and Mr. Anchorman? Even Mr. Doran? Had they made it out? She scraped at the snow as panic bit at her. She was the reason they were all here, on this mountain. They wouldn't have been caught in the snow if they hadn't followed her.

She dug faster though her fingers burned with cold and her cheeks stung with tears. Scoop by scoop, she cleared snow from around Caleb's head, then his broad chest, which barely rose and fell. She shook his shoulder, but he didn't wake. His body pinned her in place, so she kept digging to free herself. Finally, she could maneuver out from under him and gently rested his head on a pile of snow.

She stepped over him and dug out his torso, though she could no longer feel her fingers. Nor her toes. Cold wrapped itself around her as sweat dripped down her temple and back. Her teeth chattered.

Yet, she made progress one handful of snow at a time as darkness encroached. Until, in the last bit of light reflected off the falling snow, she saw the red snow packed against Caleb's stomach. A gut shot.

No, no, no. She pressed her hand against his side, squinting in the darkness to see whether blood still flowed. It had stopped, but there were other concerns. How much blood had he lost? How to keep him warm? How to get him down the mountain without the horses?

She eased him onto his back and sat on her heels. Exhausted and numb, her mind whirred too slowly.

Help me, Lord. She shook Caleb's shoulder. "Please wake up. I can't manage this on my own."

No response. She checked his breathing. It was shallow, but it meant he was still alive. She leveraged herself to roll him partially onto his side in order to see the damage. A through-and-through, thank God. And not center gut, so there was a chance. If she could keep him warm ... get him home ... fend off infection.

Tears stung her eyes. "Caleb, please. I was wrong to leave. Two are stronger than one. We need to work together. Don't leave me here alone."

But he didn't stir.

She leaned over and kissed his lips. "I love you, Caleb. Now, I need you to fight. For yourself, for me, for us. Do you understand?"

Though Caleb didn't respond, Sallie felt her words settle into her soul. She would fight for them, too. And that meant finding a way off this mountain.

She hated to leave Caleb, but staying by his side like a fluttering female would do neither of them any good. Sallie was a daughter of the mountains. As such, she'd fix her mistake. She had to.

With determined strokes, she brushed the snow from her buckskin trousers then waded through the snow toward the debris field left behind by the avalanche. The snowstorm had nearly blown itself out, and now gentle flurries fell amid gusts of light snow. Clouds broke up overhead, allowing moonlight to set the snow sparkling like a thousand diamonds.

Dangerous, yet strong and breathtaking. The mountain's heart of beauty in all its winter glory. She inhaled the fresh air, cleaned by the snow and wind, and let her eyes wander the leveled path. She had a rope and plenty of evergreen branches ... could she create a travois or sled to glide down the mountain?

"Sallie!" A voice. She looked across the open plain. Carl Anchorman.

She waved. "Can you help me with Caleb?"

The young cowboy traversed the space. "Boss okay?"

"Shot, unconscious. We need to get him to a doctor." Sallie paused. "Mr. Thomas? The others?"

Anchorman grimaced. "Thomas is trying to find them. We have the horses secured. Duke and Gunpowder?"

Hope sprung. He had horses. "I sent them away."

Anchorman tipped his hat up. "All right. Let's get you and the boss home."

Home. Warmth filled her, yet she tempered it with reality. If they could get Caleb through this, she planned to convince Caleb she didn't want to go anywhere else.

•❦•❦•❦•❦•❦•

Caleb opened his eyes. The dim light hurt, but he needed to follow the sweet humming. It was a sound he hadn't heard before. Strike that. He'd heard it in his dreams.

"Caleb!" Sallie leaned over him and placed gentle fingers on his forehead. She wore her hair back in a knot, and her usual buckskin clothes covered over her slender frame. "Finally. Your fever broke this morning."

As if swimming through sludge, he raised his hand to hers. Her soft, cool skin felt so refreshing to his crusty self. She was a fresh spring breeze after a long winter. Wildflowers and sunshine and every lovely thing ...

"You had us worried." The concern in her tone had him pushing away the poetic words that filled his mind. He tightened his hold on her. What if she were but a mirage that could vanish if he blinked?

Sallie let him keep her hand as she used her toe to nudge a chair closer to his bedside. In fact, she seemed to tighten her grip on him, as if not wanting to let *him* go. He sighed.

Would that they were married so he could pull her beside him, wrap her in his arms, lay a kiss on her neck ... he turned his face away so she wouldn't see the heat that burned there as his thoughts got ahead of him.

Then he realized they were alone. In his room.

He whipped his gaze to hers. "Sallie." Her name came out a croak.

"Easy." Compassion poured from her. "What do you need?"

"Your reputation." Why did everything feel so ... difficult? He needed to protect her yet he couldn't move.

"Don't you fret about that. I'm perfectly safe." She kissed his forehead, then nodded toward the open bedroom door. "Young Anchorman has taken his role as guardian and chaperone quite seriously. He hasn't left the hall unless Mr. or Mrs. Thomas relieves him. Anyway, Mrs. Thomas left mere moments ago to bring up soup."

"Good. I don't want to harm you." He sank into the mattress.

Turning his head, he spotted the kid as he peered into the room. Anchorman gave him a salute, then a wink. Humph. Chaperone *and* matchmaker. The kid deserved a promotion. He'd make sure Thomas—

"Oh, Caleb, I'm so sorry." Sallie leaned an elbow on the mattress beside him, yanking his attention to her.

Surprised at her sadness, he froze. "Sallie?"

Her eyes melted like snow come springtime. "I was wrong to leave the ranch. Two are better than one. I was scared."

"You, scared?" He searched her brown eyes, never imagining that emotion in her. She'd worked with Arion, a beast of a horse, without fear. She'd faced Doran, the mountain, and the snow.

Memory washed over him. The bullet wound, the avalanche, the—mercy, she saved *him*! Courageous was a much better word to define her.

He willed his dry mouth to cooperate, to allow him to speak, but she lowered her lashes.

"I'm sorry I put you in danger, Caleb." Her voice an uncommon whisper. "I thought I was in the right, that I was protecting you. But maybe I was just too scared. Maybe I'm not all that different from the horses I want to help."

He wished he could sit up to hold her proper-like. Confounded weakness. "You were coming down the mountain when we found you." *We* ... obviously, Thomas and Anchorman had made it out of the avalanche alive. Did Doran or anyone else?

Pink tinged her cheeks. "Faced with the storm, your ranch seemed the safest place for me to be."

"Here's the soup." Mrs. Thomas bustled into the room. "Oh, Caleb, you're awake. Carl could have warned me."

"Sorry, ma'am." Anchorman didn't sound apologetic. Perhaps he should reconsider that promotion ... "Boss was concerned for Miss Sallie's reputation."

Okay, he'd give the kid that.

"Of course he is. Caleb is an honorable man." Mrs. Thomas set the tray on the empty chair opposite Sallie. "How's the side?"

Caleb ignored Mrs. Thomas's attempt at a compliment. Frankly, he didn't feel all that honorable right now, considering how much he wanted Sallie all to himself. "I feel like I'm encased in dried mud."

Sallie chuckled. Mrs. Thomas laughed outright.

"Probably because we used pastes and compresses to eliminate the infection," Sallie said. "You've been out of your mind for several days now."

"Days?" He looked from one to the other. A rock sank in his gut. Time to find out the full extent of what happened. "What of Doran?"

Sallie tightened her grip on his fingers.

Mrs. Thomas shook her head. "My Mr. Thomas tried to find him after the avalanche, but there was no sign of him. All our cowboys came home safe, though. Except Erman, the traitor. He skipped town before the storm."

"Again, I'm sorry I put you and your men in danger, Caleb." Sallie cast her eyes to her lap. "I really am. It's my fault you nearly died."

"It wasn't your fault." He raised his arm, feeling the stretch of his injured side.

He pushed through the pain, needing to comfort her, needing her to see his sincerity. A tear slipped down her cheek and he growled—confounded weakness!

"Sallie, listen to me." Sweat beaded his forehead as he reached for her. "Do you hear me, darling?"

She gasped, then firmed her lips. "Don't you try to sit up, you will pull out your stitches."

He glared back. "Doran wanted to kidnap you. He followed you. That was his choice."

"But what about you?" A tear slipped down Sallie's cheek, and her chin trembled. "I almost lost you."

The pain was too much, and he relaxed against the mattress. "I would give my life for you, Sallie. I love you."

Her mouth formed a perfect *O*, and he couldn't deny himself any longer. He tugged her toward him, and she fell with a hand to his chest. Inches from his gaze, he took in every beautiful thing about her perfect face.

"How I love you." Her eyes squeezed closed as he cupped her cheek, and another tear slid down. He wiped it away. Then, he eased his fingers behind her neck and urged her closer. His side screamed, or he'd have risen to meet her. Instead, she dropped her lips onto his.

Sweet, beautiful heart.

After a blissful moment, Mrs. Thomas cleared her throat. Sallie sat back with pink cheeks that only made him grin.

The older lady shook her head. "Let's get some food in you, Mr. Caleb, then Sallie and I will let you rest. I'll have Mr. Thomas help you bathe later."

There was no stopping the red on his face at that statement.

"What?" His cook's eyes twinkled as she fussed at his blankets. "We need you smelling nice so you can court this beauty properly."

"About time!" Anchorman called from the hallway.

Sallie covered her face, but her shoulders shook, and laughter tumbled out.

Caleb couldn't help but grin. "Sounds like a plan to me."

Chapter Fourteen

Spring was getting the upper hand as the calendar closed in on May. Except for today. Flurries sprinkled through the air like sugar. Sallie breathed in the chill air, then patted Gunpowder's neck, more content than she'd been in ages.

"I don't think this will turn into a storm." Caleb halted Duke beside her, then looked up at the mountains. The memory of the avalanche still caused a shudder to slither through her. For all her time following Papa around the wilderness, she'd never been so close to one, never almost died in one.

"Ready to head back?" she asked him. This was his first excursion away from the ranch since the gunshot and fever. She watched him closely for any sign of fatigue.

His eyes twinkled at her. "Let's stop here for a few minutes." He crossed his wrists on his saddle horn. Duke nosed the frosty ground for any grass. Ever since he'd awoken from the wound-induced fever, he'd been ... different. Lighter. Happier. Flirtatious, which was an odd word to describe such a large man.

Sallie copied him, and cocked her head. "You have something on your mind."

"I do, but ..." He glanced at her, concern in their depths. Caleb had lost a lot of weight in his recovery, not enough to take away from his breadth, but his cheekbones appeared sharper over his newly trimmed beard. Handsome, yes, but the way his compassion shown through his gruffness never failed to touch her heart.

"You know you can tell me anything." She'd barely left his side over the last couple of weeks, and he'd opened up to her. It felt like unearthing a treasure. They'd talked about everything and nothing, about horses and cattle, and even their growing up years.

But one thing they hadn't discussed was the future. What would happen when her father returned? With Doran still missing, his threats still hovered, so she couldn't quite relax.

Caleb returned his gaze to the peaks. "Do you want to return to your cabin in the mountains?"

She sucked in a breath. This question mattered to him, and he didn't want her to know. Yet, how could she not? It was evident in the tension of his shoulders, the way his throat convulsed under his beard, and in the tightness of his voice. He was asking because he cared about her despite being afraid of her answer.

Sweet, lovable bear of a man.

But they'd promised to be honest with one another. "I will always miss being on the mountain. It's where I grew up." She kept her tone circumspect, not giving away too much because she was also afraid. Afraid the hope building in her heart would be dashed.

He turned to her and held out his hand. "Tell me the rest."

Of course, he noticed her discomfort, just as she'd noticed his. He continually put aside his comfort for her.

She put her hand in his and bit her lip. "But I love working with Arion and the other horses."

While Caleb recovered, Sallie had brought Arion to the place of tolerating a saddle. He didn't like it, but he didn't shy from it either. He enjoyed following her around as she worked with the other horses. Unless there was a lady horse for him to court, of course.

She hid a smile in her shoulder. Caleb and Arion had much in common there as well. Few days went by when Caleb hadn't left her a quote, a book, a flower, or some other token to remind her of him.

Caleb stroked a thumb over her knuckles, drawing her back to the present. "Are the ranch and the horses the only things you'd miss?"

This is what she'd been afraid of, though. These growing feelings between them. They were like an untamable fire, an avalanche of emotion. She knew Caleb had marriage on his mind, but she felt as skittish as the foals she'd also been working with.

Young Anchorman had shown a unique talent for reading a herd and guiding his horse where he needed to be before he needed to be there, so Sallie noted what the horses needed to know so she could train the colts. It was invigorating work that spoke to a future on the ranch that called to her more strongly each day.

But ... she had no example of what a wife was to be. She had no social graces. What if she embarrassed Caleb? The thought of it made heat bloom on her cheeks, and she glanced away.

"Sallie." He tugged her arm, and she turned to him again. Somehow, he'd urged Duke closer to Gunpowder so that the two geldings pressed side by side. Caleb leaned across the minuscule space between, eyes intense. "Enough implying, Miss Beauregard, I'm straight asking. Would you miss me?"

"Of course, I would." She slapped the back of her hand against his rock-hard chest to fight off the nerves creating havoc in her stomach.

"Sallie." He cupped her neck, drawing her closer. His eyes searched hers. "Because I would miss you. I love you, Sallie. I want you to stay on the ranch. As my wife. If you'll have a beast like me."

"Truly?" She covered her mouth as emotion swept over her. He'd said he loved her, showed he thought of her, but ... "What if—"

"Stop." He tugged her hands away from her quivering lips. "What did you teach me? Love casts out fear, Sallie, and I love you."

Tears filled her eyes. "I love you, too. So much. I—"

His lips stopped her words, and she leaned into him. Falling deeper in love with this amazing man.

Or was that her body falling? She squeezed her thighs around Gunpowder's flanks, pressed her toes into her stirrups. Realized she was completely off balance. Gunpowder responded to the pressure of her legs and stepped forward. Sallie broke away from Caleb's kiss and squealed as she tumbled.

"I got you." Caleb's chuckle rumbled through her as he held her suspended by the waist, his arm hooked around her middle. "A month ago, I could have swept your legs up. But my gallantry will have to wait."

Flustered, she wiggled for Caleb to set her on the ground. He obliged and she whistled for Gunpowder. He trotted back to her and nuzzled her neck. "Not your fault, boy."

"Entirely mine." Caleb winked.

"Beast." Sallie muttered, biting her lip against a grin as she remounted Gunpowder.

"Beauty." Caleb's face broke into the biggest smile she'd ever seen on him. Wrinkles fanned from his eyes, yet he looked younger as joy sparkled in their brown depths.

"Hey, boss!" A cowboy from the ranch waved his hat over his head as he galloped toward them. "Visitor on the ranch for you."

Sallie's stomach tightened. Had Doran survived and returned?

"Who is it?" Caleb asked as Duke trotted to meet the cowboy, Sallie and Gunpowder close behind.

"Miss Beauregard's father, sir."

Excitement at seeing her father mingled with nervousness. Did Caleb mean his offer of marriage? What if her father took exception? What if—she closed her eyes. *But Caleb loves me, and I love him.*

"Tell Mr. Beauregard I'll be along shortly," Caleb told the cowboy. As soon as the man turned away, Caleb intertwined their fingers on Gunpowder's saddlehorn. "Sallie, this is good timing. I'll ask him proper for your hand, if I may."

That's when she realized what truly scared her. Not being married. Not being Caleb's wife. She desperately wanted her father's approval to marry the man she loved. "Do you think he'll say yes?"

"Don't worry, my love." He kissed the back of her hand. "I don't surrender."

No, he certainly did not, but neither did her father.

·❣·❣·❣·❣·❣·

Caleb wiped his palms on his trousers as he paused outside the open library, where he had earlier welcomed Mr. Beauregard. The reunion between father and daughter had been sweet. He'd watched for a few moments, then took his leave to let them talk.

While he'd waited for his chance to speak to her father alone, he roved from barn to stable to pasture. A path he hadn't taken much since Doran shot him. Not because of the injury, but because he wasn't as restless as before.

Sallie brushed by him, and he couldn't resist swiping his fingers against hers. Pink bloomed on her cheeks. Her father cleared his throat. *Oops.*

Or not. Might as well let the man see how much he loved his daughter.

"I'll be back with tea." Sallie glanced over her shoulder at her father, then darted away.

He'd shown a brave front to Sallie, knowing how much it meant to her to have her father's approval, but he couldn't deny the nerves that prickled his skin. The old trapper had entrusted his daughter to his care. That didn't give him leave to fall in love with her. Would Beauregard see Caleb as a cad or give his blessing?

And if he refused, what would Caleb do? He couldn't be a wedge between father and daughter. Had he known Beauregard would return so soon, he might not have declared his intentions to Sallie that morning. Yet, he'd barely been able to hold back that long. He couldn't bear the thought of her leaving the ranch. Leaving him. He wanted to love her, cherish her, for the rest of his days.

"Get in here, Orson." Beauregard stood in the center of the room, arms crossed. "When I asked whether you'd been good to her after the rumors I heard in town, she told me you proposed."

Sallie! Caleb barely resisted a groan. He squared his shoulders like a soldier and marched to receive his due. "I should have told you first, sir. I'm sorry. I got ahead of myself this morning and—"

"Girl's eyes were sparkling like gold." The old trapper's eyes narrowed like Caleb imagined he looked as he tracked his prey. "It didn't take but a nudge to get her to spill the truth."

"Really?" The hopeful word slipped out, and Caleb cringed. He wasn't a schoolboy. He was a man with scars, both inside and out. Would Beauregard think him good enough for his daughter?

"You truly mean to marry her?" The demand in his question had Caleb snapping up his head.

"I love her, sir." With all his heart and soul.

Beauregard advanced on him. "And the rumor that she was compromised?"

"Doran." If that man ruined his chances with Sallie ... Caleb clenched and unclenched his fists to ease the anger. "Sir, I regret that her reputation has come under scrutiny. I assure you, I treated her with the utmost respect and decorum. She was never without a chaperone. I would not do that to her, sir."

"Because you love her." Did the man's frown soften? "I know she loves you, that's obvious."

"I'll be good to her, sir." Caleb stepped toward him, determined to convince Beauregard of his feelings. "I will look after her, provide for her, protect her. I—"

"I know." Beauregard cracked a smile. "Why do you think I left her here in the first place?"

Wait a minute. "What do you mean, sir?" Then why the interrogation?

"Sal wasn't going to meet a husband following me through the wilderness." Beauregard shrugged and paced toward the bookshelves. "With her in Doran's sights, I needed to get her married off as soon as possible. I'd heard plenty about you from Ahanu. I knew your reputation, your character. That horse of yours gave me the perfect excuse to play matchmaker."

Caleb sank onto the sofa. "Did you tell Sallie?"

"Girl turned bright red. Said she didn't think her old man had a romantic bone in his body." The man laughed. "She was too young to know the happiness between me and my wife. I want that for her, and I believe you two can have that together." He pinned Caleb with a glare. "Was I right?"

"Yes, sir. I hope so, sir." Caleb scrubbed his face. His old scars ached. So did his new one. "You really believe I'm the man for your daughter? And you thought so from the beginning?"

"I did, and I still do." Beauregard stepped in front of him. "You saved her from Doran and you protected her with your life. Thomas told me everything."

Caleb made to stand. "Sir, I—"

Beauregard held up a hand to keep him seated. "Are you sure you should be up and moving? If you split open your guts, my daughter will have both our heads."

Caleb's lips turned up at that. Never mind that he'd managed to ride this morning. But Sallie's father didn't know that.

Beauregard sat in the nearby wingback. "I also have news of Doran. Man didn't survive the avalanche."

Caleb rested his elbows on his knees. His good humor gone in an instant. He'd killed another man.

"Didn't have a bullet in him." Beauregard's words didn't help the sick feeling in Caleb's gut. "He simply miscalculated. Got caught in the snow. Not your fault. You saved my daughter."

Caleb looked up at the trapper. "I still feel responsible."

"That's because you're a good man, Orson." Beauregard considered him for a moment. "Still want to marry my daughter? Knowing I put her here with less-than-honest intentions? Knowing now that Doran is no longer a threat?"

Caleb squared his shoulders, his side aching from today's activity, but he forced his torso straight. "Absolutely, sir. My love for her has no condition."

His future father-in-law grinned. "Hear that, Sal, my girl?"

Sallie peeked into the room, her beautiful face full of sunshine, and not a tea tray in sight. Had she been listening at the door? He wouldn't put it past her.

Caleb held out a hand to her and started to rise, to meet her. His side pinched, keeping him seated. Yes, he overdid it today, but wouldn't have changed a thing. Sallie hurried forward, slipped close beside him on the sofa, and threw her arms around his neck. His arms came around her and he closed his eyes. *Thank you, Lord, for this undeserved blessing you have brought into my life.*

"Ask me again, Mr. Orson," she whispered. He pulled away to see her eyes. "Now that you have my father's blessing, ask me again."

He glanced at Beauregard, who nodded before he slipped out the door.

Caleb eased off the sofa, down to one knee. He clasped her small hands in his large ones, his heart full. "Sallie, my love, would you marry me?"

"Yes, yes, a thousand times, yes." Tears shimmered in her eyes, then she captured his lips in a kiss.

Epilogue

June 21, 1921

Fifty years later ...

"You really think this kid will be a good addition to the ranch?" Caleb paced the library, wanting to get this interview over with so he could finish preparing for his anniversary supper with his wife that night. He had yet to set up the phonograph.

He grinned at the thought. He'd gotten a new suit just for dinner, had his youngest granddaughter purchase a new recording disc of Sallie's favorite song, and knew just the cutting of fresh flowers to get once he'd freed himself of this obligation.

Yes, fifty years married to the best woman he knew was something to celebrate. Fifty years of raising two daughters, and now four grandchildren, on a ranch he could only run with her help. Mercy, he loved her.

"Kid reminds me of myself when I was his age." Carl Anchorman, grizzled from years of outdoor work, gave a definitive nod as he stood in the library doorway.

What were they talking about again? Oh, right, the cowboy looking for a job. Anchorman had run into him in town that morning and convinced him to come to the ranch. Convinced Caleb to offer the kid a job. Was that a firing offense? Should be.

"And look how you turned out," Caleb growled. "Inviting random cowboys here on my anniversary."

He was only semi-serious, and Anchorman knew it. In all honesty, the kid had been his most loyal cowboy and was the obvious choice to become foreman when Thomas passed away years back. He had absolutely no doubt that every one of Anchorman's decisions were with the Orsons' and the ranch's best interests in mind. He'd staked a lot on it, and Anchorman had never failed him.

"I told him to show up at one." Anchorman jabbed his chin at the mantle clock. Ten minutes till.

Caleb had an insistence about punctuality. "If he doesn't show up in the next five—"

"Minutes, then he doesn't get the job." Anchorman flashed that grin of his. Irritating man. "I know, boss."

"I don't think you need to worry about him being late." Sallie swept into the room like a fresh breeze in her light blue dress. She only wore trousers when riding now, not that she looked any prettier either way. Gray hair, wrinkles? Still his beautiful woman.

He reached a hand out for her and she tucked herself into his side. Why had he let Anchorman convince him to honor the interview? In fact, why had he agreed to an anniversary dinner? They could take two horses and disappear to catch the sunset.

"My dearest husband?" Sallie was laughing at him.

He raised a brow. Her cheeks pinked. He might be in his 70s, but he could still flirt and there wasn't anything he liked better than seeing that rose color bloom on his Sallie's cheeks.

She swatted his chest. "A cowboy just secured his horse to the hitching post out front."

He sighed. "And?" He trusted his wife's judgment of character most of all, and if he had to meet the cowboy, he might as well get her blessing now as later.

"Made sure he was here early enough not to lather his horse with galloping. Loosened the girth after he hitched him to the post. I even caught him giving the horse a few extra pats." That was instant approval in her mind, and she'd never been mistaken.

A knock at the front door and Caleb strode toward it before Anchorman could move, though he was reluctant to leave Sallie behind.

"Be nice, my love," Sallie called after him.

Caleb grunted. He'd mellowed with age, or so he thought. Still, most people were intimidated by his size, even now that he looked more like an old man with his frizzled gray beard and leathery face. In some ways, they were more scared of him now than in his younger years.

The young man on the front porch swept his cowboy hat from his head when Caleb opened the door.

"Afternoon, sir. Ma'am." He peered past Caleb's broad shoulders for a moment, and Caleb felt Sallie's hand on his arm. "Mr. Anchorman said I might apply for a job."

Caleb studied the kid—was he twenty?—for a full minute, noting that he didn't squirm under the scrutiny. He had a deep, calm voice, though the way he squeezed the brim of his hat said he was nervous. He had on Levi's, worn boots, and a clean shirt. But what struck him most was how the kid's broad shoulders nearly matched his own. An ache spread in Caleb's chest ... with his close-cut beard and brown eyes, this kid could have been his own grandson.

"Reminds me of someone," Sallie whispered, reading his mind as she had for over half a century.

Only the kid on the porch didn't have shadows in his eyes like their Ben did. Caleb refocused on him. Skipped over introductions to keep the pressure on. "What brings you to Blue Spruce, young man?"

The cowboy raised his chin and squared his shoulders. "Big brother has the family home well in hand back in Wisconsin, so I sought out work to send money back home."

But Caleb caught the wanderlust in his eyes because he'd seen it when he looked in a mirror. Until the war. Free to roam because all was well at home.

"Mr. Orson, I presume. I heard you're a fair boss. Last place, not so much. Looking for a new place to work hard."

Interesting. Caleb didn't expect the kid to interview *him*. He could respect that, liked that he used his name and pushed for a proper introduction.

"And ma'am, felicitations on your anniversary. I—"

Anchorman appeared on the porch, obviously having gone out the back door and slipped around in time to stop the kid's explanation. The red on the man's cheeks said he'd set the interview for today, not the kid. Caleb raised a brow at his foreman even as Sallie was chuckling beside him.

"He comes highly recommended, boss." Anchorman folded his arms.

"We'll see about that. Might need a new foreman after this stunt," Caleb grumbled. "Now if you have a problem with a man kissing his wife, wait for me in the barn."

"Oh, go on with you." Sallie pushed him away before he could claim a kiss. "And don't be such a beast."

Caleb reached over her for his hat and used the excuse to wrap his arm around her waist. He grinned a second before he stole a kiss.

"I'd say it was their anniversary," Anchorman was saying behind him, "but this is a normal occurrence."

The kid chuckled. "I can only pray that someday, maybe I'll find a love like that."

Caleb broke the kiss and Sallie pushed at his chest. Her look echoed his thoughts, that maybe this kid actually would be a good addition to the ranch. Caleb settled his hat on his head, and the kid did the same, with a nod to Sallie.

"Can't promise anything, but let's see what you've got." Caleb held out his hand. "What's your name, son?"

The kid shook with the strength of a man. "Silas Ward, sir. I appreciate the opportunity."

·♥·♥·♥·♥·♥·

Sallie set her book aside and rose from the sofa where she'd been reading while Caleb interviewed the young cowboy. She approved of Mr. Ward, but a man of good character could still be an ill-fit on the ranch—that decision she'd leave with her husband.

She climbed the stairs to their room, anticipation rising although her bones protested the damp air. Being nearly seventy added unfamiliar aches and pains each day, it seemed. She'd push through them, though, because she'd planned an extra special supper to celebrate fifty years as husband and wife.

The yellow dress she'd had made special for tonight called to her. She no longer had her figure from her youth, but with a few nips and tucks, the dress was the most flattering dress she'd worn in a long time. It reminded her of those days before they were married, of courting as winter turned to spring.

A lifetime ago.

Soon enough, the clock struck seven in the evening. Her stomach fluttered with excitement. Yes, she was still in love with her husband after all these years. Fifty years of joys and sorrows. Of building a family, and losing them, too. Horses had come and gone as well.

Storms and snow nearly devastated their herd. Economic downturn and strong profits. Together, they'd faced it all.

They had two beautiful daughters, one of whom was now in heaven, and three granddaughters, who all lived on the ranch with their widowed mother. And then there was their grandson, Benjamin …

The summer he turned eighteen, he was falsely accused of murder. The poor boy didn't stand a chance against his accuser, what with that criminal of a father, no mother, and a grandfather everyone still feared. And so Benjy had run and they hadn't heard from him since.

She whispered a prayer for God to bring him home, still believing him to be alive, though with each passing year of silence, the doubts grew. She dabbed at the tears that escaped each time she thought of the dear boy, a near spitting image of his grandfather when she'd first met him, then gave herself one last look in the mirror before descending the steps.

"There's my beautiful wife." Caleb stood at the bottom, waiting for her and looking handsome in a new blue suit and trimmed gray beard. He'd cleaned up after the interview. Before she could ask how it went, he held a hand out to help her down the stairs. "The house is all ours now. Cook left supper on the table. And the girls are all out for the evening."

Sallie couldn't help but giggle. Big strong Caleb, surrounded by so many females. He grinned at her as she reached the last step, then swept her into a twirl so that she landed against his chest. He kissed her soundly, one arm snaking around her waist as it always did.

"My love." He rested his forehead against hers and danced them toward the dining room, where a waltz played on the phonograph.

After her father gave them permission to marry, she learned her husband was a true romantic. Rarely did a day go by when he wasn't secreting her away to watch a sunset, tugging her outside to dance in the rain, or racing her to the mountains on their horses.

She rested her head against his chest, as she did every time they danced. She loved listening to his heart. His arms closed around her and she sighed with a deep contentment she never could have imagined all those years ago.

"Fifty years." He kissed the top of her head.

"I love you, Caleb. I don't know how it's possible, but I love you even more now than the day you proposed."

"I feel the same." He tightened his hold on her. "Because you, my darling, are my heart. My heart of beauty."

·♥·♥·♥·♥·♥·

Silas Ward is the hero of
Refuge for the Archaeologist
\#
Benjamin Ford is the hero of
The Recluse's Vindication
Read on for an excerpt

HEART OF BEAUTY

·❤·❤·❤·❤·❤·

The Recluse's Vindication

Thursday, April 27, 1933
Scottish Highlands near Fort Augustus

Benjamin Ford stood atop a hill cloaked in a mist that hid him from God Himself and his fellow man. Head bowed under the weight of his sins, they pressed on his broad shoulders. But he would carry them if it meant an innocent would live.

The cool dampness swirled around him. The lapping of Loch Ness below created an otherworldly sense. There was life beyond the veil. Today, he didn't want to acknowledge it. Perhaps because yesterday, he'd taken a thirty-fourth life. The exact number of years he'd lived on this earth.

Or maybe because today heralded the sixteenth anniversary of the first time he killed a man.

What absolution could there be for a man with so much bloodshed on his hands? He opened them now, his sleeves rolled to his elbows, revealing the tattoos gained from his time in the US Navy. Droplets formed on weather-worn skin, the mist heavy with water. It couldn't wash away the darkness that threatened to crush his soul.

"Herr Ford?" a tiny voice preceded the equally tiny child.

"Yes, Amalie?" Benjamin switched to German before kneeling before the brave little orphan girl he'd smuggled out of Germany last night. Her blond hair hung limp about her pale face. "Are you ready to see Miss Blair? She'll have tea and biscuits."

"Will I like my new home?" Her blue eyes shimmered. The poor girl had lost so much in a few short hours, stolen by men who thought her Jewish blood made her less than they. "I don't want to leave you."

"Oh, wee one." His voice roughened as she slipped into his embrace. He had promised her father, his friend, that he would do all in his power to protect the man's only child. But she deserved more than the damaged soul of the likes of him.

Benjamin clenched his jaw against the anger that welled within him. Abe Klein and his wife were good people. Amalie's father, a university professor, helped bring peace to his country after the Great War, which is how Ben first met the man. Then, earlier this year, Chancellor Hitler was elected and turned the government inside out, and Abe turned to providing intelligence to the Brits, using Ben as a go-between.

Amalie whimpered, and Ben pressed her head against his chest. When word came that Jewish children would no longer be allowed to attend school, Abe planned to send his wife and daughter to Scotland with Ben while staying to fight against the coming evil.

Only, Ben was too late for his friend and his wife. He'd had to kill to save Amalie, then whisk her and the information her father died to protect out of Germany.

For this innocent child, he hadn't hesitated to do what had to be done. He couldn't hesitate now. He tugged Amalie so he could see her tear-stained face. "Miss Agnes loves children, you know."

"Will I stay with her?" The little girl swiped at her cheeks.

That wasn't the plan, but Ben reconsidered as he used his massive thumbs to catch two errant tears that sped down her cheeks. "Shall we ask her?"

Agnes Blair was a wizened, elderly lady with contacts within US and British intelligence most would never believe, and the reason he'd lived on the edge of Loch Ness these past ten years. Technically, he worked for the US military. Still, should he be captured smuggling innocents and information out of countries like Germany, Italy, and Russia, he'd be disowned and left to face likely execution. Not that he cared. He was expendable.

"I wish I could stay with you." She rested her tiny hand on his, and his heart cracked. What had he done to deserve the trust of this child?

·❤·❤·❤·❤·❤·

Continue reading
The Recluse's Vindication
daniellegrandinetti.com/the-recluses-vindication

·♥·♥·♥·♥·♥·

From the Author

Dear Reader,

Thank you for joining me for Caleb and Sallie's story. This is my first retelling and my first story set outside the Depression era.

This novella originally released as part of the Hearts of the West multi-author collection. When I considered joining the collection, I wondered how I could fit my brand of story into the parameters: a story set west of the Mississippi River sometime in the late 1800s. I'd finished writing Silas Ward's story in *Refuge for the Archaeologist,* and a lightbulb went on. Why not tell the story of the ranch where he used to work?

From there, Caleb and Sallie's story blossomed like spring flowers. From Caleb Orson (whose name literally means "loyal bear" to Sallie, whose last name is of French origin and means "beauty." Doran's first name is Brenden, which means king or prince, which seemed completely fitting. Sprinkling in a reclusive father, a pair of ranch hands, and all the fun twists and turns of the *Beauty and the Beast* ... this proved one of the most fun tales to write.

When I got to the end and a new cowboy appeared on the ranch? I giggled with glee! If you haven't read Silas Ward and Cora's story yet, you can find it *Refuge for the Archaeologist.* It's book two in my Harbored in Crow's Nest series, however, you don't have to read book one to appreciate Silas's story. Find out more at daniellegrandinetti.com/refuge-for-the-archaeologist.

And then Caleb and Sallie's grandson, Ben? The young man appears as the hero in The Recluse's Vindication, a pre-WWII historical romance. Though part of the Our House on Heather Wynd multi-author collection, it can be read as a stand-alone. Discover why the Loch Ness Monster isn't the only recluse seeking a Scottish haven. Find out more at daniellegrandinetti.com/the-recluses-vindication.

Many thanks to the people who helped bring Caleb and Sallie's story to you. My friend and critique partner, historical romance author Ann Elizabeth Fryer. My editor, Sarah Hinkle, and second editor, Bethany Aich. My cover designer, Madisyn Carlin. My Early Reader Team, Fireside Ballyhoo team, and all the amazing readers who have encouraged me throughout this process. And, of course, My husband, Gabriel, my real-life hero, and my boys, who think having a mom who writes books is so cool.

Thank you again for reading *Heart of Beauty.* If you enjoyed it, would you consider leaving an honest review on your preferred retail site? Reviews are a great way to help support your favorite authors and their books.

I'd love to keep in touch. The best way is via my weekly Fireside News email. As a thank-you, new subscribers receive a complimentary ebook. Sign up here: daniellegrandinetti.com/fsn.

I thank God for readers like you.

Danielle Grandinetti

Historical Note

If you've read my stories before, you know I write 1930s historical romantic suspense. So when the opportunity to join this multi-author series, I knew it meant stepping out of my comfort zone. But I'd just released *Refuge for the Archaeologist,* in which Silas Ward was the hero, and knew I had to tell the origin story of the ranch he considered home. What better way to do so than write a *Beauty and the Beast* retelling?

While I've visited the Rocky Mountains many times, I have never ventured into Montana. Fortunately, my husband has a good friend, Tyler Wilkens, who lives there and who offered to tell me all about it. The surprise snowstorm and barn roof collapse are thanks especially to him. So, thank you, Tyler, for helping bring this story to life! It meant so much! Any creative licenses that would never occur in Big Sky Country are all mine.

Another huge thank you goes to my my Aunt Valerie, horsewoman extraordinaire. She taught me from early on that if I wanted to ride a horse, I had to take care of it. I learned to clean hooves, give a good brushing, and properly cinch a saddle. Though one particular pony managed to keep enough breath in her belly so that the cinch wasn't as tight as it should be and I nearly tumbled off her neck on the way down a ravine. This led to me riding bareback up that steep path, which may have inspired certain parts of this story. Auntie Valerie also read the first few scenes with Arion so I could more accurately show his escape and the gentling process. Any mistakes are solely due to me being a greenhorn.

The late 1800s was a tumultuous time in Montana Territory and I couldn't write a tale set then without mentioning the horrible actions that caused so many members of the Blackfeet people to lose their lands. While I cannot personally undo the atrocities, I hope by having a hero honor that land through a charge to protect others, I, in turn, might offer honor and respect to their stories. To learn more about the history of the Blackfeet Nation, and the people who call themselves "Niitsitapi" (nee-itsee-TAH-peh) meaning "the real people," you can begin at the University of Montana website: https://www.umt.edu/this-is-montana/columns/stories/blackfeet. php

Join my Fireside News

Grab a spot on my virtual hearth and receive a weekly email filled with bookish content. As a thank you for subscribing, you'll receive a digital copy of my historical romance novelette: *Fire and Water*.

Subscribe Here

Our House Novellas

As the world marches toward what will become WWII, visit Our House as we join the resistance.

The Italian Musician's Sanctuary
Romance, history and intrigue at Our House on
Sycamore Street.

Hunted by one man, can she open her heart to another?
Eden Cove, England, 1931—Margherita Vicienzo flees Italy
pursued by her former fiancé, a member of Mussolini's Blackshirt.
Smuggled illegally into England, Margherita is a foreigner at the
mercy of strangers. Her limp from an improperly healed broken
leg means she has nothing to offer the Ferryman family, who offer
her sanctuary, and nothing to appease their son who resents her
presence.

Luke Ferryman needs a wife. He wants to marry for love, but
carries the weight of his family's generations-old expectations on his

shoulders. Though he inherited the role of both baker and ferryman, he knows he can't fulfill both needs once his aging grandparents retire. A wife would help, but not an illegal one like the refugee his matchmaking grandmother is harboring.

As opposite as night and day, Luke and Margherita forge a tentative friendship that grows despite the constant threat of Margherita's discovery. But when strangers appear in the close-knit seaside town, threatening Luke's livelihood and Margherita's safety, the choice between justice and mercy becomes harder. And sacrifice proves the only answer.

The Recluse's Vindication
Rumors, Monsters, and Second Chances at Our House on Heather Wynd

The Loch Ness Monster isn't the only recluse seeking a Scottish haven.

Bieldfell, Scotland, 1933—Falsely accused of murder sixteen years ago, American cowboy Benjamin Ford has chosen to hide out in the Scottish Highlands. Reclusive and not afraid to die, he rescues children out of an increasingly dangerous Germany. When his childhood best friend appears at his door, he's not the boy she remembers.

Eleanor Finch's life ended sixteen years ago. In one horrible day, she lost her dreams, her reputation, and her heart. However, she never gives up the hope of finding her friend, so when she learns of

Ben's whereabouts, she leaves all that is familiar to convince him to return home.

But Eleanor isn't the only person searching for Ben. Hunters follow her trail. The thin veil of gossip and rumor may be their only chance of a future ... unless the Loch Ness Monster is real after all.

daniellegrandinetti.com/our-house

Harbored in Crow's Nest

Welcome to Crow's Nest,
where danger and romance meet at the water's edge.
daniellegrandinetti.com/harbored-in-crows-nest

Confessions to a Stranger

Harbored in Crow's Nest, #1
She's lost her future. He's sacrificed his.
Now they have a chance to reclaim it—together.

Refuge for the Archaeologist

Harbored in Crow's Nest, #2
Will uncovering the truth set them free
or destroy what they hold most dear?

Escape with the Prodigal

Harbored in Crow's Nest, #3

*Only a Christmas miracle will save
an unwed mother and the lumberjack protecting her.*

Relying on the Enemy

HARBORED IN CROW'S NEST, #4
*She's protecting her children.
He's redeeming his past.*

Sheltered by the Doctor

HARBORED IN CROW'S NEST, #5
*A fake relationship might keep her safe,
but will it break their hearts?*

Investigation of a Journalist

HARBORED IN CROW'S NEST, #6
*A second chance to set the record straight,
and rekindle a lost love.*

Fairytale Retellings

Heart of Beauty

stand-alone origin novella

Discover the origin of Crooked Tooth Ranch in this 1870s western retelling of Beauty and the Beast.

daniellegrandinetti.com/heart-of-beauty

His Boss's Little Sister

stand-alone novella in the Apron Strings Tea Tale multi-author series

A touch of fairy tale, a spoonful of history, and a teacup of hope … a 1930s historical romance retelling of Hansel and Gretel.

daniellegrandinetti.com/his-bosss-little-sister

176

Undercover Wish
stand-alone novella, part of the Di Stasio Giornaliste
Agency series

*A Di Stasio Giornaliste Agency origin story and a retelling of Aladdin
and the Magic Lamp.*

daniellegrandinetti.com/heart-of-beauty

Di Stasio Giornaliste Agency

La Verità con Integrità. Truth with Integrity.
The Legacy of a (Girl) Stunt Reporter.
daniellegrandinetti.com/di-stasio-giornaliste-agency

Undercover Wish

Di Stasio Giornaliste Agency, #0
Alessandra Di Stasio
Chicago World's Fair: World's Columbian Exposition

Eyewitness Sketch

Di Stasio Giornaliste Agency, #1
Gabriella Salatino
Prohibition

Sabotage Games

DI STASIO GIORNALISTE AGENCY, #2
Emma Hancock
Summer & Winter Olympics: Lake Placid & L.A.

Shrouded Trail

DI STASIO GIORNALISTE AGENCY, #3
Lena Carney
Presidential Election

Fraudulent Progress

DI STASIO GIORNALISTE AGENCY, #4
Klara James
Chicago World's Fair: A Century Of Progress Exposition

Pursuing Dust

DI STASIO GIORNALISTE AGENCY, #5
Tabitha Jóhannsson
Dust Bowl

Hostile Ally

HEART OF BEAUTY

Dɪ Sᴛᴀsɪo Gɪᴏʀɴᴀʟɪsᴛᴇ Agᴇɴᴄʏ, #6

Liesl Kaufman

Berlin Olympics

About the Author

Danielle Grandinetti is an award-winning author of 1930s historical romance, where mystery and suspense intertwine with hope. Her work has received recognition including a Distinguished Faith in Writing Award, two National Excellence in Storytelling Awards, and finalist honors in the FHLCW Reader's Choice, Selah, and Daphne du Maurier contests.

A second-generation Italian-American rooted in Midwest traditions, Danielle draws inspiration from tea, books, and the creative beauty of nature. Holding a master's in communication and culture, and driven by a lifelong love of stories, she crafts tales that celebrate resilience, diversity, and belonging. Danielle lives along Wisconsin's Lake Michigan shoreline with her husband and two sons. Find her online at daniellegrandinetti.com.

www.ingramcontent.com/pod-product-compliance
Lightning Source LLC
Chambersburg PA
CBHW021708190726
48289CB00008B/2436